All Eyes
on
Tommy Gunz

Warren Holloway

AMERICA'S NEW STORYTELLER

GOOD 2 GO PUBLISHING

ALL EYES ON GUNZ

Written by Warren Holloway

Cover Design: Davida Baldwin – Odd Ball Designs

Typesetter: Mychea

ISBN: 9781947340275

Copyright © 2018 Good2Go Publishing

Published 2018 by Good2Go Publishing

7311 W. Glass Lane • Laveen, AZ 85339

www.good2gopublishing.com

https://twitter.com/good2gobooks

G2G@good2gopublishing.com

www.facebook.com/good2gopublishing

www.instagram.com/good2gopublishing

PROLOGUE

Listen up, America. I'm about to take y'all niggas on a tour of my life and how shit unfolded in the corrupt city of Harrisburg, Pennsylvania—the capitol filled with corruption and crime. From one city to another, real recognize realest. So, allow me to introduce myself. I'm Tommy Guns, a goon's goon, a hustla's hustla, and also a gangsta's gangsta. From yo' hood to my hood, welcome to Corrupt City.

All Eyes on Tommy Gunz

CHAPTER 1

May 2006

IT WAS CLOSE TO eighty degrees outside in Harrisburg, Pennsylvania, with the sun shining. The ladies were out showing off their bodies in the shortest come-get-me shorts, with Nubian skin glowing from the oils, lotions, and body glitter they placed on their skin to enhance their beauty.

My city was also known as "Corrupt City," since the laws were made here. It was filled with corrupt government officials, along with corrupt niggas chasing the real American dream—that cocaine money.

I'm Tom "Tommy Guns" Anderson. I'm the realest nigga you'll ever meet. The ladies love my six-foot medium-built frame. The niggas in the street fear my presence and dark stare. Or maybe it's the Glock 40mm they know I'll pop on their ass just 'cause.

I was coming down 6th Street in my G-500 Benz truck with custom platinum-painted 23-inch Lexanis and pitch-black tint, beats banging. My cousins, Big Ivan and Ace, were in their whips behind me stunt'n hard. Big Ivan was in his BMW 745Li. Ace followed in his Audi S6. Big Ivan was Ace's big brother. It was always family for me. We stayed strong before this getting-money shit, and now we couldn't be stopped. This was our city. The only one missing from this family was my big cousin, Jim Gotti. He got caught with five hundred pounds in '97. He'd be out in 2009. The Feds had him sitting in FCI Gilmore down in Virginia. His books stayed tight.

I pulled over at 6th and Forest seeing these sexy-ass sistas coming out of Jay Jay's barber shop. That nigga was trapping on the low, so he keept some nice pieces in and out of that spot.

Soon as I pulled over, my two goons from Allentown jumped out of the truck, staying at my side and ready to ride for whatever. Big Ivan and Ace jumped out of their whips posting up against their shit as if they were in a rap video or something.

I crossed the street, and all eyes were on me, but my eyes were focused on the baddest bitch I had seen in a long time. She was in the middle of the other two sexy chocolate pieces.

"Yo, lil momma, come here. Let me holla at you!"

She turned my way with a smile, along with her girls she was with. Her smile was official, but it was her soft, honey-brown eyes that were even more alluring. She was standing about five foot one with curves everywhere—a whole lot of fun.

"You smiling, you know I'm talking to you," I said as I closed in on her, coming face-to-face. "What's your name?"

"Tamia, but my friends call me Bright Eyes."

She was cutting her eyes at my whip and then back to me while checking out the $10,000 Breitling watch with flawless diamonds in the face. My bracelet matched the watch. My chain was diamond encrusted with my sons' pictures in it. As for my clothes, the shit I wore on Monday was what niggas were wearing at the club. I had popped these tags this morning on this Sean Jean T-shirt and jeans, flowing with my official baby-blue gator print Air Force Ones. I ordered them exclusively online.

"I'm not even gon' play around with you, baby girl. I'm trying to take you out of town and have fun with you."

She didn't even ask who I was, because she knew already. Uptown was my hood, and Harrisburg was my city.

She was smiling from ear to ear. Damn, she was making this easy.

Before she could respond, I saw a look in her eyes that displayed instant fear. Right at that moment, I heard gunfire erupt from behind me.

I turned quick only to see one of my Allentown niggas falling to the ground from a pounding head shot.

I moved quickly, ducking behind a Toyota Camry as I pulled out my Glock 40mm. My other nigga from Allentown was firing off at the two young niggas that were shooting my way. I guess I took somebody out they knew. Either that or they were trying to take my spot. Whatever the case was, I wasn't going out like that. I raised up and unleashed slugs in their direction.

"I got you, cuz!" Big Ivan's voice boomed through the air as he popped the trunk on the BMW, grabbing the 12-gauge riot pump. Ace reached into his S6 and grabbed the MAC-10 he had tucked behind the passenger's seat.

Them little niggas came strapped, and they gunned down my other Allentown goon. They were firing with two guns apiece, one in each hand.

Shit changed quickly when my cousin came unleashing the thunderous riot pump. That shit was shaking everything from the sound and brute force as its bullets crashed into the cars around it.

Them little niggas took off running after seeing Ace and Big Ivan coming with their shit. I couldn't have that, so I came to the corner popping off. My slugs raced through the air downing one of them niggas. The other kept running. Ace ran behind that nigga, chasing him into an alleyway, firing off but missing him as he turned the corner.

The little nigga on the ground was lying in the middle of Forest Street. Ace ran down on that nigga, standing over top of him.

"You a stupid nigga trying to get at my cuz like you built for this shit!"

"He killed my dad and tied my mom up when I was ten. Fuck you niggas!"

Ace pulled the trigger only to hear a click, signifying that the gun was empty. At the same time, police could be heard in the distance.

"Yo, Ace, five-o," I yelled, trying to make sure he could get away.

Big Ivan also called out to his baby brother, making sure he didn't get caught up.

I drove off, not wanting to stick around for the heat. Big Ivan did the same, racing off swiftly in the 745Li.

~ ~ ~

Ace was mad that his gun was empty, so he kicked that little nigga in the leg that I shot him in, before sprinting back to his whip.

As soon as he got into his whip, he mashed the gas and pulled away from all the drama and the crime scene with my two out-of-town goons.

The cops pulling up saw Ace pulling off fast, which made him an instant suspect. They raced behind Ace, not knowing he was skilled at driving.

Ace was scared because he couldn't get caught. This life we were living was too good to go to jail on some bullshit like this. He was putting all his skillz into weaving in and out of oncoming cars. The cops didn't want to jeopardize the children out playing or any other innocent pedestrians, so they slowed down and called in other officers in the area.

Ace saw the cop slow down, so he was feeling himself.

"That's what I'm talking about!" he yelled out, with his foot still to the gas feeling the power of the V-10 engine.

His excitement was short-lived when he spotted two cop cars pop out from the side streets trying to corner him. Right then he switched over from automatic to manumatic, putting the 500-plus horsepower to use.

He turned hard down Schuylkill Street and made his way toward 7th Street. He darted through the stop signs, turning right and mashing the gas down 7th Street doing 100 down in a 35-MPH zone. He came to 7th and Maclay Street at a green light, turned left onto the Maclay Street Bridge, and opened it up, accelerating to 110 down to Cameron Street. There he caught the green light leading to the bypass and taking him on the Hillside.

The cops didn't see Ace turn on the bridge, so they continued racing uptown looking for him. Ace made his way onto the Hillside, where he parked his whip on a down-low street before calling Big Ivan.

Big Ivan picked up on the first ring after seeing

that it was his baby brother.

"Baby bro, you good?"

"You already know they can't fuck with my driving skillz."

"Where you at now?"

"On 19th and North."

"Leave your whip there. I'm on my way to come get you."

"Alright."

It didn't take long for Big Ivan to get to Ace. He was also on the Hillside. As soon as Ace got into the car, he was still hyped up from the shit that just took place.

"Them little niggas is crazy, bro! He better be glad that clip was empty."

"They must think shit is sweet, but we didn't get here the easy way, and we ain't about to lie down for none of these clowns out here."

~ ~ ~

I didn't know where my cousins were at, so I hit them on the phone to make sure Ace got away safely.

Big Ivan's phone rang once before he answered.

"G's up! What's good, fam?"

"Them stupid-ass young niggas are fucking shit up and making us hot. Yo, is Ace good?"

"Yeah, he good trippin' on his driving skillz."

"Them niggas still looking for me uptown, cuz," Ace said in the background, always the hyped one.

"Yo, let's link up over at the McDonalds by the high," I said, knowing they already knew what spot I was talking about.

I didn't want to give too much detail over the jack in case we had listeners.

"We en route right now, cuz."

Big Ivan stood six foot two, weighed 240 pounds, and wore braids in his hair. He had light skin and a full beard that he kept trimmed. He was always about this money shit, plus he would tie a nigga up in a heartbeat if they fucked with his money, food, or family.

Ace, my little cuz, was the baby boy of the crew, but he always was ready to ride. He loved them guns, getting money, and them white bitches across the river. He was a real hood nigga with a baby face, brown skin, and a low-cut fade on the sides. He stayed in shape and would dust a nigga in a straight-up fight, too.

With Ace and Big Ivan behind me, we couldn't be stopped, and when my cousin Jim Gotti came home, shit would be all the way *la familia.*

CHAPTER 2

I WAS IN MY whip sitting behind the dark tint at the Kline Village Plaza waiting on my cousins, so we could politic about this call I just got from one of my out-of-town customers.

Big Ivan pulled up smooth in his 745Li, hitting the switch on the dark tinted windows and exposing their faces as he pulled up to the side of my truck.

"What's good, cuzo?"

"The homie from York, PA, trying to grip a little heavy, so I want you and fam to come through with me. You know we got to keep shit all the way official, especially after them little niggas tried to get at us. I feel like they want the position and power we got."

"Fuck them little niggas, cuz. That one better be glad my shit was empty, or I would have left him there!" Ace snapped quickly.

"Ace, find out who those niggas were, and make sure you put somebody on them, so they don't even think about doing stupid shit like that again."

"I'm on it, cuz, but let's take care of this business

first."

"Ivan, I need you to stop past the spot and grab four of them money makers, and then meet me behind the college in one hour."

"I'm on that now, cuzo. See you then," Big Ivan said, pulling off as he hit the switch to conceal him and Ace behind the dark tinted windows.

I sat for a minute looking around as I always did, making sure I wasn't being followed by the Feds, or targeted by niggas trying to take me from my position. I also took that time to reload my Glock before placing it on my lap for easy access.

As I was pulling off, I took notice of two things that stood out to me.

The first was an all-black, custom-painted Brabus 65 Mercedes Benz parked beside a silver custom-painted Bentley Flying Spur. Both vehicles were well over $150,000. Being a big car fanatic, I appreciated the whips.

But it was the two Arab men leaning against them that also made me think something other than the norm. Because the only Arab I knew with money like that was Vartan.

As I was passing by the cars, I rolled my window

down to get a better look at the whips. I guess I wasn't the only one who was the paranoid type, because my staring caught the attention of both men who were speaking Arabic to one another. Their thick eyebrows added to the dark stare they were giving me. Real talk, my Glock was in my hand now ready for them to say something stupid. But they just stared. So to break the tension, I gave them a shout-out.

"Yo, I like your whips. Them joints is all the way official."

They didn't respond to me but continued to speak to one another as they were watching me drive off. I rolled my window back up to check the rear-view mirror and saw that they were still looking. Now I'm thinking that they were looking at my tag. I was thinking about turning back around to see what the fuck they was thinking, but I needed to take care of this business with my man, D.C., from York.

This nigga JD from the South Side projects, also known as the South Acres, introduced me and D.C. about a year and a half ago.

D.C. was laid back about his money and them bitches. He was a brown-skinned nigga who stood about five foot ten. He wore the 360 waves, and he kept his shit razor sharp, trimmed just like his close beard. He was thirty-two, the same age as me and Big Ivan. He was medium built and was one of them niggas that hit the gym just to check out the chicks. It was a double benefit for him.

D.C. had shit on lockdown in York. He used to cop a four and a half. He stacked his paper and hustled smart from what I had seen in him.

I made my way to the location taking the back streets, being paranoid as always. Plus, I wanted to get there a little early to check shit out.

CHAPTER 3

I WAS SITTING IN my truck backed up to the wall. Big Ivan and Ace came twenty minutes ago to hold me down. This spot was low-key and out of the way. Plus, this warehouse was vacant last I checked, so no one would mind if I occupied the parking lot for a brief moment.

I was looking at my watch seeing that this nigga, D.C., was behind schedule. He was late, and it wasn't a good look for business, especially with these four bricks sitting in fam's whip.

Fam was in his whip with the shotgun close by. Ace also was strapped and reloaded ready for whatever.

Big Ivan rolled his tint down to shout me out.

"Yo, cuz, what's good with your boy? He's never late, right?"

"Yeah, I'm about to hit this nigga on the jack to see where he at."

Just as I said that, three all-white cargo vans pulled into the warehouse parking lot followed by the black Brabus and the Flying Spur that I saw over at the plaza.

"Who dat, cuz?" Big Ivan asked, seeing the same shit I was.

"That's them muthafuckas I seen over by the high when y'all left. I wonder what the fuck they into following behind them vans and shit?"

"They got major weight in them joints," Big Ivan said while trying to be funny.

"Yeah, right! Them Arab niggas be trying to blow shit up!" Ace said before laughing.

"Whatever they doing, they doing it big by driving whips like that," Big Ivan added.

"Big bro, we doing it big, too, nigga," Ace said.

As the vehicles continued on, heading toward the back of the warehouse, the Arab men also took notice of the two vehicles parked, seeing the G-500 Benz truck from earlier.

The Arab in the Brabus two-wayed the one in the Flying Spur, probably communicating what he was thinking about the truck he had seen earlier.

They were paranoid just as I was; I don't blame them. I was paranoid sitting on these four blocks waiting on this nigga, D.C., but I couldn't really figure out why they were paranoid. They were doing something they weren't supposed to be doing. I needed to get the fuck out of here before shit went wrong; because if I was them, I would want to know why we crossed paths twice.

I knew they weren't cops; they were businessmen on a whole other level.

Soon as they passed by, I hit up D.C. to see where the fuck he was at. He was making me even more paranoid.

Just as I was dialing up his data, Big Ivan yelled out.

"Yo, cuz, is that your boy right there?"

I looked over and saw the 760Li with the V-12 engine. It was custom dark with candy-red chrome 20s with dark candy-red backdrops and red tint faded to a mirror finish. This was his new whip, and that shit was all the way official.

Big Ivan was definitely appreciating the 760Li BMW, especially being a BMW owner. It was making him want to step his game up with the big boys.

"That candy paint sets that big boy off nice," Big Ivan said, then added, "I might have to upgrade to that soon, fam."

"That could be your out-of-town toy. You know you can't really do it like that around here unless you got a business or something," I said, making sure he stayed focus.

I got out of my truck as D.C. backed into a parking space. I was pissed and ready to check this nigga about being late.

Big Ivan and Ace was already out of the whip, guns at the ready, and their eyes open for anything coming that I wouldn't be able to see.

"My nigga, Tommy Guns, what's good with you?" D.C. said as he got out and came up to me, extending his hand to shake.

I looked at this nigga heated but was ready to do business.

"What the fuck took you so long? You know you got me out here heavy?"

"I got caught up, my nigga," he responded, turning to point at this sexy-ass Spanish mami with dark blonde hair and dimples in her smile as D.C. pointed to her.

"She wanted to see how the back seats recline, so we made it happen. It was a beautiful situation."

"She from your way?"

"I met that joint down B-more at Club Diamond strip joint on Baltimore Avenue."

"That's my spot down there. Norma Jeans is also official," I said before getting down to business. "Next time, don't put pussy before paper, especially when you got a nigga on standby with four blocks."

D.C. saw the look in my eyes, the seriousness, and knew that I wouldn't hesitate to leave his ass where he stood.

"I feel you, my nigga. That shit won't happen again," he responded, glimpsing over at Ace and Big Ivan and seeing their serious faces.

"You got the paper now, or you want this up front?"

"I got bread for three of them joints, and if you want, I'll bring the cash for the other one within two days or sooner. Niggas is on a drought down there. They waiting on me."

"You good for the other one? Get the paper to me when you get it."

I made my way over to the truck where my cousins were standing. I grabbed the four bricks out of the back seat before making my way back to D.C. The Brabus 65 was leaving the property and eyeing me and my whip down before radioing to the other

Arab that remained at the back of the warehouse. That shit right there made me even more paranoid. Normally I would chase this clown down and confront him, but I was in the middle of taking care of business.

I hurried over to D.C. ready to finish up, so I could get out of here. This spot was dead. I couldn't use this location anymore, because I wasn't trying to run across these Arab niggas anymore just in case somebody was watching them.

I grabbed the bag of money from D.C. He took the bricks, jumped into his whip, and raced off. I jumped in my shit and turned the music up. Big Ivan did the same while racing off behind me and feeling this getting money shit. It was $100,000 just like that. I couldn't complain. That was a day's work. It takes a doctor a year to do that. The only risk to this job was niggas were always trying to take you from position, like those little niggas earlier. Other than that, I was loving this shit.

CHAPTER 4

A FEW DAYS PASSED by. I was up in New York with my connect, King Jose, taking care of business in the back of his bodega in Spanish Harlem.

King Jose was one of the realest muthafuckas in the game outside of me and my family. He saw something in me when I was coming up in the game. Like me, he, too, got his paper with blood on his hand. King Jose blessed me with fifty bricks consignment on top of what I was already moving. He trusted me, seeing the same real nigga in me that was in him. Besides, his goons would track me down if shit got fucked up. I wouldn't let that happen.

King Jose's uncle also gave him help in the game. He told him to die broke or on top with a smile. I think he chose to get rich. Fuck a smile.

"Tommy, I like you, *mi amigo*. You always come correct. I wish I could say the same for the other *puntas* that I give a chance to."

"Good business is a business that will go a long way," I responded while sipping on the drink he had one of his girls bring me.

The cocaine was already en route to Harrisburg. I didn't have to travel with that shit, since those days were over with.

King Jose didn't drink because he always wanted to be on point. Besides, that's how his uncle got caught slipping. He was comfortable in his position of power, celebrating too much. These bitches seduced him, and it was a rap after that. King Jose later tracked down them bitches and tortured them before killing them slowly.

"Amigo, let me know how things are with this product. I just got it in. I was told it is at least 90 percent. I don't touch it. I want it to be the best."

"The best is good for the both of us. It means more money will be made," I said while finishing my Long Island.

I stood from the plush leather chair nodding my head as I exited. King Jose didn't like to shake hands much either. His reason was that he didn't want no one to get the drop on him. He was paranoid and had seen too many movies, I think.

It didn't take long for my flight back to PA. I made sure my driver took the work away at the stash spot. Then I made calls to all my clientele, so I could unload as much of this coke today as possible. Within the first seven calls to my associates in the surrounding counties, half of the work was sold.

I was in the city out by the South Acres when I called Big Ivan to see where he was in the hood.

"G's up!" Big Ivan said into the phone.

It was something we always did when answering the phone. It was some street code shit.

"G's up, what's good with you, fam?"

"Ain't shit! I'm on the Hill pushing point uptown so I can grab some wings from the Chinese spot, Chans."

"I'll meet you up there. Get me some wings if you get there before me."

"Alright, cuz."

Chans was in the hood on 8th and Maclay Street. It was the one spot everybody in the hood ate at when it came to Chinese grub.

Big Ivan was parked when I pulled in. He jumped out of his whip into my truck as we waited on the food to get done.

"What's good, fam? I see you shining as always."

"You know how we do, cuz. If it ain't official, we can't rock it."

"Yeah, yeah. Yo, you know I was down Miami with wifey trying to put that QT in since we go hard out here. While we was down there, I came across this nigga named Turnpike Tito. He's a real boss down there."

"Yo, let's grab this grub and you can finish telling me inside," I said, feeling a little hungry.

He continued to speak once we were inside the spot.

"Yeah, this Spanish nigga was feeling my HBG swagga at this club we was at. He sent me and wifey a bottle over to our booth. So, to show my appreciation, I sent him a bottle of that King Louis XIII. You know, that expensive Hennessy?"

"Cuz, you wild, but that's some real shit."

"I ain't done, cuz. Listen to this shit. After I sent the bottle over, I made my way over to him. His security stopped me, but he invited me in, and we started politicking on a whole another level. He mentioned that he wanted to expand further up north, so I mentioned how we do up here. We exchanged data. So, whenever you want to get at him, we can make it happen."

"Is he official?" I asked, knowing how vice is

down there. They play the part, fooling most out-of-town niggas.

"He the truth, cuz."

"We can fly out in the a.m., get a face-to-face, talk numbers, and go from there."

I was all for meeting new connects even though King Jose showed me love. I just wanted to expand just as any businessman should.

We grabbed our food and made our way out of the Chinese spot, when slugs roared through the air, slamming into the closing doors and windows. I heard a slug hit Big Ivan's BMW, which I knew made him heated.

We both dropped our food and reached for the guns on our waist. When I locked up, I saw an arm pulling back inside of the white cargo van. Right then, I thought about the cargo vans I saw a few days ago. This wasn't good. I needed to get these muthafuckas.

Big Ivan jumped in his whip and mashed the gas. I was right behind him with adrenaline flowing. I was ready to kill these stupid muthafuckas.

Big Ivan caught up to them first in the fast seven series, popping off shots out of the sunroof. Slugs slammed into the back of the cargo van.

He attempted to pull to the side of the van until the oncoming traffic forced him back behind them. The van made a sharp right turn on Woodbine Street, with his tires screeching while heading toward Jefferson or 7th Street. I knew we needed to get these muthafuckas.

Me and Big Ivan were on their ass as they turned right again onto 7th Street. It was only two lanes, the lane we were in and the oncoming lane, so I couldn't go around like I wanted to. Once they got to the light, they raced through the red light, not wanting to risk getting cornered. Big Ivan raced behind them over the bridge as he popped another clip into his black steel nine. Slugs pierced the back door of the van, crashing into the driver and making him swerve. This shit was happening fast as they closed in on Cameron Street. I was thinking they were heading toward route I-81; instead, they turned toward the hood on Cameron Street with four lanes, two going one way and two going the other. There was plenty of room now.

The back doors of the van swung open with a shooter taking aim at my cousin, until he sent slugs crashing into his face and slumping him instantly. The body fell out onto the busy street. Cars ran over it multiple times before they figured out what was going on. There was one more in the van, the driver.

I raced to the driver's side, rolling down my window just as the Arab muthafucka faced me with murder in his eyes. Right at that moment, I knew he was going to try some stupid shit. He veered left hard and fast. I slammed the brakes just as my instincts warned me. The van went into the next lane's oncoming traffic as a big rig was coming 65 MPH, slamming into the cargo van and sounding off like a loud explosion. The driver was killed on impact as the steering wheel crushed his chest. The flames from the engine exploding engulfed his remains. I mashed the gas, looking through my mirror, hoping that no one was clocking our tags.

I hit fam up on the cell.

"Yo, meet me at your sis's spot on Liberty Street," I said, wanting to get cuz's views on what just went down.

He didn't even say anything. We headed to my cousin's crib. I hit Ace up, too, so I could put him onto what had just happened.

CHAPTER 5

MY COUSIN, EVA, LIVED on Liberty Street where we all linked up at. Eva didn't play the streets, but she didn't complain about the money we all gave her. Eva is Big Ivan's big sister. She could've been a model or a Janet Jackson double growing up. Only difference, her eyes were grayish. It definitely made her stand out in the hood, being caramel brown, with long black hair and standing five foot nine as a model should.

Anyway, Big Ivan took his greedy ass inside the crib as I waited outside to discuss business. My adrenaline was still racing from these crazy muthafuckas trying to take me and my cuz out.

Ace came racing down the street in his whip with music blaring. He came to a halt and jumped out, leaving the door open and making the music louder as he came over to my truck.

"What's good, cuz?"

"Ain't shit! These Arab niggas just tried to take me and Ivan out."

"You talking about that crazy shit on Cameron?

I just seen how they had that shit blocked off all crazy."

"Yeah, cuz! Them some stupid muthafuckas. They think shit is sweet."

Big Ivan was coming outside stuffing himself with a turkey sandwich.

"Look at this nigga. That's why my mom's always shopping when he comes around," Ace said before laughing. "Yo, give me a piece of that joint," Ace said, not waiting on a response while reaching his hand out to grab a piece of the sandwich.

Big Ivan gave him this look like, "This greedy muthafucka!"

"I ain't giving you shit no more, Ace!" Ivan snapped with brotherly love as he flexed and made Ace back up a little.

"Yo, when you done stuffing your face, nigga, we out to Miami to take care of the BI you was putting me on to. Ace, we gonna need you to hold it down until we get back. Dump as much, if not all, of the work. Anything jump off, get at me," I said, ready to step up my venture into this new business with this nigga Turnpike Tito.

If he wasn't who my cuz said he was, then I was

going to leave him behind.

When I got back from Miami, I was going to find out who these Arab muthafuckas really were, because it was clear they didn't know who the fuck I was.

Ace's cell phone sounded off and got his attention. It was one of his chicks hitting him up. I could tell from the look on his face, plus he was quick to put us onto the call.

"This bitch stay texting some freaky shit. She wants to give me head on the highway during rush hour. She gets off to people having the chance to see us freaking."

"That's got to be that white bitch, Anita, you brought around last week?" I asked.

"You already know, cuz. I'm out, cuz!" Ace said, pounding up.

"Stay on top of business, not them hoes," I said.

"I make money; then make time for them hoes. Pussy only pay when you pimp'n," Ace said with a smirk, before getting in his whip and racing off.

My little cuz was definitely thorough and about his money. He was also a playboy when it came to the ladies.

"Big Ivan, we out in my whip."

I'm ready to take care of this new business. I always kept travel money in my armrest. Twenty stacks were also enough to get away fast and far before the cops or any law enforcement would have a chance to catch up. Big Ivan, like me, had money, too, but he always made sure he didn't starve. Plus, he liked spending money in the strip clubs and going to Miami. We made it rain down there.

We headed to the airport and booked a flight on the first thing smoking. Once we got on the plane and headed to the Sunshine State, a drink was needed. I got a shot of Hennessy, while Big Ivan opted for vodka.

"Toast to going down here and coming out on top with a good business deal," my cousin said.

"To family and good business," I said, always wanting to put family first.

We downed the shots before politicking about the crazy day we had thus far.

Hours passed by, and the skies cleared as the plane descended into Miami. Palm trees and beautiful women set the scene. There were Latinas and white bitches with golden tans and blonde hair.

We saw slates with caramel flawless-skinned bodies with curves. The smiles were welcoming, even the women working in the airport.

"Yo, cuz, this is where it's at."

"Wait 'til we go to the clubs," Big Ivan responded.

"Call that nigga Tito, and let him know we here," I said, wanting to put a face to this fly-ass street name.

He sounded like he was in position, but vice could make some niggas believe them, too. If he was vice, he better have had the drop on me, because I'd choke the shit out of this nigga and take his gun. Shoot him with his own shit.

My cuz hit this nigga Tito on the jack. I guess he didn't recognize the 717 area code at first, since he didn't pick up right away.

"*Quien es ese?*" he asked, not knowing it was my cuz.

"Big Ivan from PA. We-!"

It came to him; he remembered who cuz was.

"Mi amigo, I remember Big Ivan. We met at the club."

"Yeah, that's me. I flew in just now with my cuz

I got at you about."

Turnpike Tito already knew what it was hittin' for.

"My friend, let me finish up here with this beautiful *blanquita*, and I call you back."

"I'll be waiting on your call," Big Ivan said.

I knew that nigga Tito was either trying to make sure we were official or was setting a trap. Either way, I was thinking just as fast as he was if he was even thinking like me.

We made our way to the Miami Hilton and checked into a suite. We ordered some food and got clothing to stunt for tonight after taking care of this business, if we even had time to do that. I was more focused on business.

An hour passed by, and this nigga Tito hadn't called yet.

"Yo, cuz, what the fuck is up with your boy? He got us on standby like he forgot about a nigga."

"He was with some freak when I called him earlier. She got him whipped."

"If he a boss like you say he is, that bitch was off of him the minute you hung up. He probably making sure we are who you said we is. Either that or he vice."

"Tommy, why would you say some shit like that? You trying to make me paranoid, cuz?"

"Options, always keep them open. Therefore you'll run into less surprises, nigga."

Big Ivan's phone sounded off. It was Tito. Cuz pointed to the phone before answering. Tito gave cuz instructions on where to meet. He even sent a limo to the hotel. How he knew that we were here was another thing I was trippin' on. Truth be told, I was leaning more now to him being a boss and cautious about who he was dealing with, especially having us meet him at the Miami ports.

The ride in the limo was quiet. We were both thinking about this business deal while at the same time keeping our eyes open. It was the level of paranoia kicking in being in this business; besides, the day we had so far didn't help.

As the limo pulled into the port, driving around before coming to a slow halt, I noticed two all-white H2 Hummers. Each flanked the sides of the sky-blue Lamborghini with the white leather interior.

Me and cuz stepped out of the limo. Simultaneously the doors to the H2s opened as four

Latinos from each Hummer exited. They were all strapped with fully automatic weapons. They stood close by the Lamborghini where Turnpike Tito remained before leaning over to this sexy-ass Puerto Rican mami with silky black hair and blonde highlights. Her light brown skin was glowing. She had a smile and lips that made you want her to suck you off.

This nigga, Turnpike Tito, is the real deal. He stepped out with his swagga turned on, shining with white linen pants and a sky blue short-sleeved silk shirt unbuttoned at the top, exposing the diamond necklace he was wearing with the Virgin Mary encrusted in diamonds. The eyes on the Virgin Mary ware blue diamonds. His watch was just as flawless, flowing with the pinky ring and bracelet.

Turnpike Tito stood six foot one with a slim build. He was a Puerto Rican with a Miami tan. His dark hair was combed back, and he looked the part of a true Miami kingpin.

His face was clean, and his eyebrows lined up with a razor that added to his Latino flare of perfection. He spoke with a Spanish Miami accent. He was real smooth yet displayed his position of power.

"*Que paso, amigo?* My apologies for having you wait so long. But as you know, I have to make sure everyone is who they say they are."

As he said that, two of his men came over to me and my cuz to search us for weapons. I didn't trip. It only allowed me to know he was even more official than I originally thought. King Jose was boss, but this nigga seemed to be in an even better position just by the way he was carrying himself.

"Now that these muthafuckas is done searching us, you want to talk business?" I said, still remaining true to myself and gangsta.

Turnpike Tito smirked before speaking. "*Espera un minute, amigo.* Business is coming. Tommy Guns, right?"

"Yeah."

"*Tu familia* tells me good things about up north."

"We surviving and making it happen. Right now, I'm trying to see if you can make it better."

"Hermano, we need to give you a little help, so you can be comfortable in your position instead of just surviving."

"What's the numbers on the menu?"

He glanced over at my cousin and then back to me.

"You buy fifty or more, 13.5, and I'm not talking cheap shit. You can cut this shit three times and still have grade-A *cocaina*."

Damn, that's a good number right there. But why settle for the first thing he threw out there to me. Plus, it's only business-like to negotiate.

"Twelve five is the going rate here in Miami. So, you telling me I come all the way from PA to be charged an extra $1,000?"

I didn't know what the going rate was. I figured I'd shoot that out there. If he bit, then it was on him.

This Turnpike Tito nigga was serious. I saw it in his eyes as he stared me down. I didn't budge. I was just as serious as this nigga was. The only difference, he had his team with guns. I had my cuz, even though he would ride out no matter what if this Turnpike Tito nigga was feeling disrespected by my counteroffer.

"You know, *hermano*, normally I would think you were trying to be greedy, but you came to do business. I respect that, because I see if things go well today, we'll have a promising future of business." He paused then said, "Okay, 13 even. You're smart enough to know I won't budge any lower."

I extended my hand to shake on the deal.

"Thirteen it is, amigo."

"I can have that ready before you leave town."

"We outta here in the morning," Big Ivan said.

"No problem, amigo. Also, if you buy fifty, I'll front you fifty. Like I said, I see good business in you; besides, I have your information. It is a part of me securing my best interests, which is my business and myself."

Like I said, this nigga, Turnpike Tito, was the real shit. He was on some smooth Scarface-type shit.

I already had 600 stacks on vacuum seal up north. I just needed to hit Ace up and put him on to this next day air shit.

I made the call to little cuz, and he picked up on the second ring.

"G's up."

"G's up! What's good, cuz?"

"Making it happen on my end," Ace said.

"I need you to next-day air six vacs down to my hotel suite."

"I got you, cuz."

"Did that nigga from York get at you?"

"Nah, he moving slow."

"I'ma get at him later. Make sure you secure that soon as we hang up and stay on point."

"Always, cuz," he said before hanging up.

I focused back on Tito talking about this money, so he would feel comfortable doing this deal. I wanted to show him how I move.

"Yo, I'll have that paper in the a.m."

"My friend, I will see you *mañana*. Until then, enjoy my city," he said while turning and getting back into his super-fast Lamborghini, revving the engine before racing off with the Hummers following behind him.

CHAPTER 6

BACK AT THE MIAMI Hilton, me and my cuz were putting that shit on for the night ahead. On the way back from the ports, Turnpike Tito hit up Big Ivan and invited us to Skyblue, a well-known Miami spot, and also a club he owned.

After, I did a little checkup on Turnpike Tito, along with what I already knew after meeting him face-to-face. He was the real thing. He was also backed by a more powerful force, his big brother, Tony. They call him El Fantasma, or The Ghost, because he's always in the background or never seen. But his power and connections to the most powerful people in the world made him even more of a figure to be respected. I'm glad my cuz stumbled across this nigga because I see a promising future with him.

Once I was official in stunt mode, I was ready to make another business call to make sure my shit up north was still going right. Plus, I needed to check on this nigga D.C.

As the phone was ringing, I stood looking out of the floor-to-ceiling window at the Miami powder-blue skyline that was beginning to fade into the night. Yeah, this was the American dream at its best. I got fifty plus fifty of the finest blocks of raw. Money was never gonna be funny fucking with King Jose and this nigga Turnpike Tito. I'd lay a nigga out to protect this position and feeling of power I felt right now. Just as this thought was running through my mind, D.C. picked up.

"Tommy Guns, what's up, my nigga?"

"That paper. Everything official on ya end?"

"Ready when you ready."

"I'm a send my fam to get at you, so be on point."

"You already know," DC replied as he hung up ready to get this paper. I hit up Ace, and he picked up on the second ring.

"G's up. What's good, cuz?"

"G's up, you little nigga. I need you to get at that nigga D.C. for me."

I paused after hearing this bitch in the background moaning, so I knew right then Ace wasn't focused on what I was talking about.

"Ace, what the fuck you doing, nigga? I'm talking about this paper while you fucking around!"

"This Spanish mami was all over me before you

hit my phone. She was heated, so I was finger popping her to going until I got off the phone with you."

My little cuz was definitely wild. He loved them bitches, and they definitely loved him and all the excitement he was bringing into their lives.

"Focus, cuz. Get at D.C. and handle that. He'll be waiting on you to get at him right now, alright?"

"I'ma put this pussy on pause so I can take care of this BI for you, cuz," he responded.

He must have stopped because mami was in the background calling him papi and begging for him to keep doing what he was doing. He did the right thing; business was first. She would wait; and if she didn't, there was more just like her and better.

"Now you focused. That's what the fuck I'm talking about, cuz. Now get at that 717 data and handle that BI."

"I see you when you get back, cuz."

After the call, me and Big Ivan poured a drink from the minibar in the suite. A drink well deserved after having a successful business day and meeting another real nigga, Turnpike Tito.

We knocked the drinks back ready to pour

another, when we heard a knock come across the suite's door.

Big Ivan gave me a look that was like, "What the fuck?" I was thinking the same thing.

"You order anything, cuz?" Big Ivan asked me.

"Nah, nigga, you see I was on the jack," I said as I was on my way to the door, not knowing what to expect. "Let's see who it is."

When I came to the door looking through the peephole, I started laughing after realizing how paranoid this drug game can make a nigga. If me and Big Ivan were strapped, we probably would have had our guns cocked and ready.

"What the fuck is so funny, nigga?" Big Ivan asked with a confused and paranoid look on his face.

"I'm laughing because it's two bad-looking bitches on the other side of this door. One of them is that bitch that was in Turnpike Tito's whip earlier."

I opened the door already knowing what they were there for. This nigga Turnpike sent them over showing his Miami boss hospitality.

"What's up, papi?" the Spanish mami said with a glowing smile that matched her radiant skin. She was also the one that was in the whip with Turnpike Tito.

"I'm Chica, and this is Ariana."

Ariana was also a bad bitch, standing five foot ten with a pair of Jimmy Choo heels on. The white dress was short, hugging every curve on her body, especially the 36Cs that were perky. They were probably fake but real to the touch. Nipples pressing up against the dress added to her appeal, giving a show for those looking. Her lips were glossy, which added to her natural yet exotic Russian look. She had glowing blue eyes, and her Miami tan flowed with her platinum blonde hair. Both of these bitches were iced out, thanks to Turnpike Tito.

"Come on in. I'm Tommy Guns, and this is my cousin, Big Ivan."

"Big Ivan, yes?" Ariana said caressing my cousin's arms then his stomach. "You a boss like Rick Ross?" she added, making her statement funny with her sexy, soft Russian accent.

Cuz gave a smooth laugh while rubbing his own belly.

"Yeah, I'm a boss. You already know. Turnpike Tito don't fuck with niggas that ain't on the same shit as he is."

Both of these bitches smiled knowing that cuz

was right.

"Papi, we have a Mercedes Benz limo awaiting us downstairs."

"Chica, what's the rush? Take this drink with me and my cuz," I said, wanting to pour that second drink me and cuz was going to have.

"One drink, papi. Just so you know, jefe don't like when shit don't go his way," Chica said, referring to Tito as the boss.

Me and cuz were drinking shots of Patron Platinum before they came, so I figured we'd continue with the same bottle and pour these fine-ass bitches a shot.

I filled the glasses before we all raised to toast.

"To a good night!" Chica said, with a salacious look in her eyes.

I didn't know what to think. Was she was Turnpike Tito's main bitch, or did she do whatever he sent her to do? We downed the shots ready to start the night, but Ariana wanted another shot.

"One more and that's it."

She was looking at me and then my cuz. At first I was going to deny her just in case these hoes was trying to test a nigga. Then I caught another look from Chica as if she wanted to bypass the shots and suck me off or something.

"This is the last until we either get into the limo or to the club," Big Ivan said, thinking the same as I was, wanting to be on point and not too sloppy in front of this nigga Turnpike Tito.

The second shot was actually me and Big Ivan's third, but the second for these bitches. I was good. I could drink half of this bottle and still be focused enough to lay a nigga down, or these bitches if they started acting stupid.

As we started for the door, Chica placed a light caress on my arm accompanied by another look. Then her grip closed on my arm as she pulled me closer. I didn't even think about resisting her soft-looking lips. My hand made its way to her soft hips before wrapping around to her plush ass. I squeezed it, which set off a light moan, but that was the extent of this because she pulled back and looked into my eyes.

"Now, now, papi, we don't want to ruin how the night could end."

She was good at being a tease. It made me want this bitch even more. When I turned back around,

Ariana was gripping Big Ivan's dick through his pants, wanting to fuck as his fingers caressed her clit.

"Yo, cuz, let's go. That's gonna be there all night," I said, ready to meet up with Tito at the club.

The all-white S600 Mercedes Benz limo awaited us.

It didn't take long before we made it over to the club. The lines were long. Women were on one side and men on the other; plus, the VIP line. I wasn't about to wait in any of the lines since we were on some boss shit, and we were invited by the boss.

I knew Tito was there, as I saw his Lambo out front parked alone on the curb.

Chica and Ariana were at our side as we approached the front door where the security stood. At first as trained to do, the security was about to pat me and my cuz down, until a voice of power came from behind.

"Don't you put your fucking hands on them! You see they're with my girls. I sent for them," Turnpike Tito said, coming to the door wanting to check the lines and see how business was going.

He could have done it from his office, but he was a hands-on business nigger.

"Tommy and Big Ivan, come on in and let's have some fun tonight."

We followed behind him as Chica and Ariana left our side to join his side. I was trippin' on that shit for real.

"I hope you two are ready to celebrate and eat, because I have it all here tonight. I even had mi mama in the kitchen cooking a special meal for just us. So, mi amigos, enjoy," Tito said as we entered the VIP suite secured above the dance floor, which allowed us to get a glimpse of everyone downstairs while enjoying the affluent lifestyle of a boss.

Puerto Rican soul food was the spread, along with drinks, bottles of champagne, liquor, and women from all nationalities. Everything and everyone was there to entertain us.

I bit into the fried pork chops with a little hot sauce. This shit was good.

"Tell your ma she did a good job, Tito. These chops is definitely official." Big Ivan was also fucking that shit up. When it came to food, women, and getting this money, that nigga would make sure he ate first.

The exotic bitches in the suite were nibbling on

food trying to be cute, plus they didn't want to ruin the sexy-ass clothing they were wearing. They were trying to look their best in that they wanted to be kept and chosen.

Turnpike Tito's VIP waitress came over with a bottle of champagne and glasses for me, Big Ivan, and Turnpike. She popped the bottle and filled our glasses before we turned to the balcony of the suite overlooking the dance floor. It was a packed house, full of beautiful bitches from all over. Tito made sure for every nigga in the club there was at least four or five sexy-ass chicks, most of them looking for boss niggas, while the others were independent lady bosses enjoying the Miami nightlife.

"Tommy, Ivan, mi hermanos. I'm glad we were able to do business. I look forward to more of your business, good business," he added, turning his face away from the dance floor and making eye contact with me and my cuz. "I live for this shit. Which means I'll die for this shit. You fuck me over, and I'll hunt you down and kill you, your family, or anyone who is in my way of getting my money or *cocaina*."

He wasn't loud. His delivery was simply laid out on the table as any real nigga in his position.

Normally I would be offended, but I always brought the same to the table when it came to my money and cocaine.

"Bad business to me is like being a faggot or a rat; and being a real nigga, I don't want to be associated with either of the two. So, trust that, with me, you'll always have good business. More important, you'll always have your money."

I responded by making full eye contact and showing this boss nigga that I was just as much a thug and a boss as he was. He knew, just like I knew, that he was the real thing.

A smirk came across his face as he spoke.

"Toast to good business, the good life, and a good night."

We raised our glasses as Young Jeezy blasted throughout the club, which set the get-money mood even more.

The night was going good, with drinks, food, women, laughter, and more talk of future business.

Before we knew it, it was 2:00 a.m. Although the club was closing, there was no rush for our exit since we were with the boss of Miami as well as the boss of Skyblue.

"Tommy and Big Ivan, you like my girls here?" Tito asked, referring to Chica and Ariana.

They were at his side looking sexy as if they were in a rap video. The only difference between the life we were living and the music videos was that we didn't get a second chance for any mistakes, whether it be the cops chasing us, FBI, the niggas trying to shoot at us, real bullets, and the product, tons. It was all real, and enough to send a nigga away forever.

"They definitely sexy just as the other bitches up in here."

He came with a more direct answer when speaking to Chica this time. "You want to show mi amigo a good time?"

She gave me that look again before kissing him on the cheek.

"Yeah, papi, I'll have fun with him," Chica responded.

"What about you, Ariana?" Tito questioned.

She lit up with a smile loving my cuz's PA swagga.

"He's like a teddy bear, why not?"

Ariana kissed Tito, and then both of them stood and made their way over to me and my cuz.

"I'll see you two a little later this morning, so enjoy the hospitality," he said while standing up ready to roll out.

Other females looking just as sexy as Ariana and Chica came to his side to quickly fill the void.

We made it out to the limo and back to the suite where shit got real hot.

Chica came out of her clothes in one seamless movement while Ariana followed. I was in my bed, and cuz was in his bed. Chica came over and placed her lips on my dick. She worked her magic as she was looking at me with her soft, hazel-brown eyes filled with sex and passion. Shit was like I was fucking this bitch's eyes or something. She was that good. I wanted to fuck this bitch now, so I made her stop. She climbed up on me, mounting my thickness and moaning as her tight and wet pussy slid down.

"Ahi, papi, ahi," she moaned as she leaned forward a little, placing her hands on my chest.

I didn't even need to do any work other than stay hard. Damn, this pussy is good, feeling like her mouth but better. In fact, ten times better as she worked her hips while making faces. That was a sign of how into it she was. She then got going faster as she raised up and slammed hard on my dick, hitting every spot and causing her to moan and explode over and over.

"Ahi, ahi, ahi, papi, mumh, damn, papi!" she said sensually as the sensation took over, rushing through her body. She was cumming.

She tightened her pussy almost making me bust, so I rolled her over to take control of this pussy. Just as I flipped her over, cuz was pounding Ariana from behind. She was moaning loud, almost ashamed as she put her face in the pillow to muffle the sounds of pleasure she was feeling. I focused back on this good Puerto Rican pussy, placing one of her legs over my shoulder while leaving the other leg down to give me an angle to tear this pussy up.

When I started stroking her from this position, I was feeling every wall inside of her. Her moans escaped her mouth even more, becoming louder and more passionate. Her pussy was contracting as she exploded over and over. I was liquored up and pounding this good pussy.

"Put my leg down, papi!" she pleaded sexually, wanting me closer to her.

I did as she pleased, digging deep into this good-

good. She wrapped her arms around my back, her nails grazing my back in almost a scratch. Crazy thing, that shit was feeling good until I started going hard and deeper, and then she started scratching for real.

"Hold up, Chica! That shit don't feel good right there."

"Sorry, papi, keep going," she said, with a take-me-this-is-your-pussy look.

I started back up, and this time her legs came around my waist. Instead of scratching my back, her soft lips found my neck. Normally I wouldn't let a bitch suck on my neck, but this pussy was feeling good, plus I didn't have a bitch at home, so I was good. Plus, by me allowing her to do this, it showed that I was opening up to her, or so she was thinking. She was into it. The suck mark is some possessive shit. Them Spanish chicks be on that shit.

"Mmmmmmmh, mmmmmmmh! Don't stop, papi, give it to me!"

I didn't know what it was about her words, but they did make me go harder. At the same time, I was feeling that tingling rush through my dick as the cum exploded into her body. Once I came to a halt, I wanted to get up and get clean, but she wouldn't let her grip go. She was having multiple orgasms, something her body never had experienced. Her legs were trembling, and her mouth was open. There was no sound, just light panting. Her lips quivered, and the passion in her hazel eyes sparkled. Right then I knew I had this bitch. Obviously, Turnpike Tito was the last thing on her mind.

When she was finally done, a smile came across her face before lightly punching me in the chest.

"What the fuck you do to me, papi?"

She was twisted by the dick. Now that's some funny shit.

"I showed you a good night."

I rolled out of bed freshening up, knowing the meeting with Tito would come soon as we closed our eyes.

Big Ivan fell asleep after fucking the shit out of Ariana.

I came out of the bathroom and jumped into the bed. Chica didn't hesitate to snuggle up to a nigga. I didn't push her away. She was a real bitch no matter what. She could be of good use whether it be for business, sex, or relationship.

CHAPTER 7

IT WAS 9:45 A.M. when we were pulling up to the ports in the Benz limo. Chica was at my side with her hair still wet from the morning shower. Ariana had her eyes closed with her head back, taking in the night before. Big Ivan, like me, was on point and ready to finish out this business deal with Turnpike Tito. Ace took care of business by having the money sent to me next-day air. That shit was at the checkout when we exited the hotel.

We stepped out of the limo ladies first, then me and cuz with money on our minds.

Turnpike Tito was already there with his goons in the Hummers. The only thing different was the Ferrari Enzo he was driving was custom-painted sky blue with a plush, white leather interior.

Tito was with another bad-ass bitch looking like she was Asian or something with the cat-like eyes, black hair, blonde highlights, and a model's body and stance. She was ready to ride out, and not just to fuck a nigga, but to lay a nigga out for Tito.

Chica kissed me on the cheek before she and

Ariana made their way over to Turnpike Tito's side. I laughed seeing this shit; at the same time realizing the power this nigga had not just in the game but over these bitches.

Cuz gave me a look probably thinking the same shit I was thinking about these chicks.

We approached Tito seconds behind Chica and Ariana, who were smiling.

"*Buenos dias, hermanos.* Did my girls take good care of you last night?"

"They showed us the brighter side of Miami's nightlife," Big Ivan said.

"I can't complain. The hospitality was generous," I added, catching a glimpse of Chica's eyes and emotion behind them.

She was twisted off the dick. I guess these hoes needed love too. She was a different type of ho. She was high price. The regular one- or two-brick boy wouldn't be able to touch that pussy. The dresses, jewelry, and handbags she liked cost that much. That was just a few of her lavish likings.

"Did you bring *mi chabo, hermano*?" Tito asked, getting straight to business.

The money was in a Miami Hilton bag. I turned

to get it out of the limo. When I gave him the bag, a smile came across his face once he opened it up. It was the sight of money. Better than sex to most people. A rush of power.

"This is what I like to see, mi amigo. A true sign of good business to come," he said, handing the bag to Ariana.

She took the bag over to the Hummer. She also got in the back of the Hummer wanting to rest from the night before.

"I'm looking forward to this future of good business, my nigga, along with more trips to Miami," I responded, knowing Chica would catch on to the pun intended to capture her mind and heart.

I glanced over at his whip, being a car fanatic.

"You love that sky-blue shit, huh?"

"It reminds me that the sky is the limit. So, when I'm driving, I'm looking at the sky and reaching for it at the same time, and nobody is going to stop me from getting there."

As we were talking, the men were securing the bricks of cocaine with one of Tito's associates to drive the work up north. He already knew where to go. That was info we gave Tito last night.

Once the work was secured, the driver took off first, and then we embraced with Tito once more with handshakes. He was feeling a need to reiterate his statement from last night.

"Amigos, don't forget that. I live for this shit, and I will die for this shit, so don't fuck me or my money over."

I didn't trip because he was trusting me with fifty bricks that he fronted me on top of the fifty I got from him. He wouldn't have given me the shit if he didn't think I could make his money, or if he couldn't track me down to get it.

"I'll see you in a week to show you how I get this paper, and if this product is as raw as you say it is. I'll be back for more and even sooner than a week."

"Okay, amigo, I'll see you then," he responded while turning to Chica. "Say goodbye."

"Take care of yourself, papi. Thank you for last night."

Tito laughed, hearing the passion and lust in her voice.

The Asian bitch at Tito's side was super fine. She was also eyeing a nigga down, or maybe she was on some other shit.

I nodded my head with a smirk on my face in acknowledgment to Chica, before turning back to the limo with my cuz.

Once in the limo, Tito and his crew raced off. Chica was in the other Hummer while Tito kept the Asian chick with him. He's a boss, so the bitches are going to flock to him. Chica is one of many, but loyal to him in many ways. She'd run drugs if needed or get info from other boss niggas, which made me think long and hard about this when she was telling me this shit last night and this morning. It was all a part of the business.

"That bitch was feeling you heavy, cuz," Big Ivan said.

"Yeah, she tripp'n, right?"

"Keep her at bay. It might not be good for business in the long run, you feel me?"

"Nigga, I always keep shit business first. Chica can come in good use. I just don't know for what at this time. I saw it in her eyes. She wants to be down with a real nigga like me."

"Let it play out. Don't let it play you, cuz," Big Ivan said before he yawned, tired as shit from last night partying and fucking. "I'm sleeping on the flight back, 'cause when we touchdown, it's all business."

He was right. We needed to dump the one hundred blocks I got from King Jose plus the one hundred we just got from Tito.

CHAPTER 8

THE NEXT DAY WHILE my cousin, Big Ivan, was at the crib making amends with his wifey for staying out too long without calling her, I was making moves. I secured the work from Turnpike Tito's driver. After I put that shit away, I was making phone calls to take care of business, because I didn't want to look bad coming up short with King Jose's product or Turnpike Tito's shit.

I called Ace to see where he was at, plus I wanted to make sure he was moving work as needed and not being caught up with them bitches throwing the pussy his way.

"G's up!" Ace sounded off with the G-code.

"G's up, little nigga. Where you at?"

"At Aunty's crib uptown."

"I'm coming through. I'm out by the South Acres now."

After I hung up, I turned down Hanover Street onto Cameron Street, which stretched across the city. I was making calls and reaching out to everyone down with me, meaning the niggas that got work from me.

I reached Cameron and Maclay Streets at the intersection and waited on the red light to turn green. As always, I scanned my area, checking each mirror to make sure niggas didn't try to carjack me or rob a nigga. They wanted what I had; plus, I got mine the way they were trying to get theirs, so it was a must I stayed alert.

I looked down and placed my boy's CD in. My nigga, Large Flava, was a tall nigga that be real heavy on the DJ side of things; plus, he gets it popp'n with that airtime keeping niggas on the high life.

Instinct came over me as I glanced up to see the light was still red. My eyes veered back to the rearview mirror, where I saw this Arab muthafucka approaching. My mind accelerated. I scanned the side mirror and saw a minivan pull up with the side door already ajar. Right then, the adrenaline rushed through my body as I reached for my Glock 40mm with sixteen in the box and one in the chamber ready to roll.

As I flashed between the light and the mirrors seeing their approach, I hit Ace on speed dial. He picked up on the first ring, knowing something was wrong for me to call him right back.

"What's good, cuz?"

"These Arab muthafuckas is trying to creep a nigga. Meet me on the murder."

I didn't need to repeat myself with Ace. He liked this type of shit. The Murder is a street uptown on Moore Street. It was dubbed Moore Murder after all the homicides in the early '90s.

These Arab cats were strapped with some serious metal. Shit, they had to get that exclusively.

They couldn't see my movement inside because of the pitch-black tint, but I had the drop on these stupid muthafuckas as soon as I hit the switch to roll down the window. I opened up with two back-to-back rounds that slammed into this nigga's chest and thrust him back. Then I slammed the gas, allowing the V8 engine of the G55 to push me forward.

The other Arab ran on foot behind me as if he could catch up. He couldn't, but the slugs slammed into my truck until he was hit by an oncoming cab rushing through the green light.

The minivan took off behind me as I raced up the Maclay Street Bridge to make my way into the Uptown area. I didn't know who these Arab muthafuckas was, but it was more than clear that they wanted me dead for some stupid-ass reason. It's not my time to go, so these stupid muthafuckas is getting slumped one by one until I get back to the source.

The slugs crashing into my truck sounded off loud. It was pissing me off, too, knowing these idiots was fucking my shit up.

I tried to evade the oncoming slugs by turning right onto 7th Street and making my way toward Division, with foot still to the gas, until these slow-ass cars got in front of me coming from the off streets.

"Move out the way!" I snapped, knowing they couldn't hear me, but they did hear the burst of gunfire coming from the minivan, which made them pull over quickly in order not to catch a stray slug.

The minivan came up to the side of my truck. I knew what was next, so I rammed the side of the van, forcing them all the way over into the oncoming lane. The driver reacted quickly by getting in back of me once again, still shooting recklessly as I swerved trying to prevent my truck from looking like a block of Swiss cheese.

I made a swift left turn on Division Street and headed toward 6th Street. I could see there was traffic ahead, so as soon as I got close enough, I veered into the gas station weaving around the cars until I popped back out onto 6th Street. I mashed the gas again while at the same time checking my mirrors.

I pulled away fast on these clowns, but they came back into view quickly in the minivan.

Everybody in the hood was out looking good, stunt'n, and standing around living life, until the gunfire erupted. The kids dropped down on the ground. The chicks screamed out for their kids and family members. The real niggas went for their guns.

I made it to 6th and Forest, by turning down toward the Murder. I saw Ace's Audi S6 park, so I knew he was in the cut. I stopped at Moore and Forest Streets and waited on these muthafuckas to turn into my hood.

The minivan turned onto the block fast before coming to a slow drift as if they were expecting something to go down. I was looking at 'em through my mirror. I could see 'em talking and looking at one another before they popped out of the van. There were two of them left.

They started approaching my truck, until Ace jumped out from the alley with thirty-two in the clip and one in the chamber. He squeezed off, sending five rounds out quick while tracking down the closest Arab to him. The other Arab dropped down on the side of the van, which gave me enough time to jump out. I started walking toward this Arab nigga, wanting to kill him and get an answer to why they were trying to kill a nigga. But he raised his fully automatic weapon up, until Ace came from behind, slumping him and sending his brains through the front of his skull. This shit was looking crazy. This nigga's eyes were still open like he was shocked that he got shot.

"We got to get outta here, cuz," I said while jumping back in my truck.

Ace jumped in his whip, too. We couldn't afford to stick around, especially with the amount of product I had, and the niggas that gave it to me would kill my family and reach out behind bars for their shit. I don't blame them because I would do the same, especially if a nigga went to jail and it wasn't in relation to this getting money shit.

CHAPTER 9

IT WAS 5:27 P.M., almost three hours after that shit with them Arab lames. Me and Ace went outside the hood chilling at our lay-low spot. We also called this spot the bachelor's pad, because we brought all types of bitches over here. They loved this crib's space with over 2,500 square feet filled with amenities of a balla: flat-screens, bar, stripper pole, sound system, plush leather, and furniture throughout, and each one of us had our own room stunted to the fullest. The women loved this shit.

Ace was watching the flat-screen while flipping through the channels as I poured both of us a drink. I needed this shit to take the edge off from these niggas trying to take me out.

"Cuz, look at this shit!" Ace yelled out, trying to get my attention to the television.

"Look at what, cuz?" I said while carrying the glasses back over to the lounge area. "Here, nigga, double shot of that yack," I said as I handed him his glass of Henny.

I zoomed in on the flat-screen to see that it was the news, with this pale-looking white chick reporting on what took place with them Arab muthafuckas earlier.

"I'm Sarah Jennings here in the Uptown area of the city on a street nicknamed for its multiple murders, with two more today adding to that reason the street has its name. This city is known for its level of violence, but there is no coincidence that two Arab men last week and four today have succumbed to this city's ongoing violence, leaving no true witnesses or suspects thus far. Only thing that has been reported is the weapons these men carried. Also, these men were in association with the Islamic Jihad Organization (IJO), which is in connection with the Muslim Brotherhood (MBH) that is said to derive from Egypt. Harrisburg is definitely a long way from home for these men."

Hearing the shit she was saying had me trippin'. These Arab cats were terrorists, from the sounds of it.

"Cuz, I think them muthafuckas think we saw something when we was at the warehouse. Plus, I crossed paths with 'em at the Giants. They was in them vans real heavy, looking like they was doing something. Besides, who the fuck is driving a Bentley Flying Spur and the new Benz 65 Brabus if they ain't getting some exclusive paper?"

Ace was listening and taking all of this shit in while at the same time looking back at the TV at the footage they were showing of the Arabs.

I tilted my shot glass, emptying it because it was definitely needed after hearing and seeing this shit on the news about these niggas trying to kill me.

Ace's cell phone sounded off, which immediately got his attention.

"Yo, it's that nigga D.C., cuz," Ace said, looking at the caller ID. "He gave me that paper too, cuz. I'll get it to you with the rest of the money," he added before answering the phone. "What's good, my nigga?"

"Ain't shit, other than getting mines while trying to stay on top out here. What's good with you, cuz?" D.C. asked.

"Hold on, nigga. He right here," Ace said, tossing me the phone.

"What's good, my nigga?"

"Living and trying to live better. I'm ready to change the game, you feel me?" D.C. said, referring to stepping his game up to the next level.

"Sounds good. You the third person today that's inspired by the paperwork," I said, meaning this getting-money shit.

"Oh yeah, they hungry out here, and I'm like the mission. My mission is to feed the streets."

"Say no more. We can flip that original figure."

"I can meet you halfway."

"Carwash on 7th and Peffer Street."

"I know where it's at. I'm in motion toward the city now, so it won't be long."

"I'll be there waiting. Don't waste time with them bitches, nigga. We moving heavy."

"I got it, Tommy Guns," D.C. said with light laughter as he hung up.

I hung up and tossed the cell phone back to Ace.

"Yo, nigga, mount up. We got some business to take care of. We in your whip. I need you to take me over to my other whip after we grip the work."

"I'm always ready, cuz," Ace said, standing up with his glass and downing the double shot. "Now I'm really ready, cuz. That Henny put a nigga in that mind-set."

We left the Bachelor Pad, jumping in Ace's whip and heading to the stash spot. I called Big Ivan, so he could meet us uptown at the carwash. It was a must that family was there. We knew that no matter what, we would have each other's back.

CHAPTER 10

WITHIN THE HOUR, THE bricks of raw were secured. Ace was already in route uptown checking out the carwash before I got there. If shit didn't look right, I would know before I walked into a trap.

I jumped into my new all-custom chrome CL600 Mercedes Benz, with soft black leather seats, piped-in chrome features, and chrome dials on the dash and gearshift. It was all flowing with chrome 22-inch rims. My shit even had the black tint faded to mirror tint to give my whip the added balla features.

I started my shit up sounding good, plus the power of the V-12 under the hood made my shit even more official.

I slipped a DJ Ron Ski CD in my shit, holding him down. He was a true legend in the mix CD game. Rest in peace to my nigga right there.

Ski's brother, Shawn B, came through the speakers with his hard, raspy voice spitting fire and pain in his lyrics. The beat was so hard that it put me in the business mind-set as I reloaded my Glock 40 before sitting that shit in my lap ready to get this paper.

As I took off heading uptown, that nigga D.C. was on I-83 coming across the bridge into the city. He was showing off in his whip passing cars as the BMW 760Li was gliding past each vehicle with ease. He was really feeling himself in the moment. That's how this getting real money makes a nigga feel.

He turned off at the 2nd Street exit, catching all the green lights through the Downtown and Midtown area before making his way uptown. He came down 7th Street with his music bumpin' loud with that classic B.I.G. *Ready to Die* album.

I was already parked in my whip responding to a text from Chica, the Spanish mami from Miami. She was feeling a nigga. I was also thinking that she was keeping tabs on me as her job. Turnpike Tito was that smooth yet intelligent type of businessman. Chica wanted to come up here to see how we do up north. I hit back on the text to let me handle this BI, and then I jumped out of my whip focused and ready to take care of business as usual.

Ace was inside the car wash spraying his whip down but staying on point.

Big Ivan was on his way. He got caught up with

his wifey. The home front always came first no matter what.

D.C. parked three lanes over. He jumped out the same time I got out of my whip.

"My nigga, Tommy Guns, I see you doing it real big with the new whip," D.C. said as he approached.

"My toy I had for a few weeks. It's a good look, right?"

"I wish I had toys like this when I was growing up," D.C. responded.

We both laughed at that shit, knowing how it is growing up in the hood.

"I see you keep it official with the bitches," I said, after seeing this platinum-blonde-haired white bitch with a golden tan. I couldn't see her eyes, because she was hiding them behind her D&G shades.

"I do them clubs real heavy, and this is what the outcome looks like."

I wanted to cut through the small talk because I was sitting heavy, plus Ace seemed like he was getting impatient, either that or he was just as paranoid as I was at times.

"Grab ya paper, nigga, and I'ma get these squares for you," I said, turning toward my whip. He did the same.

I popped the trunk with my remote, reaching for the bag of eight blocks. Any nigga in his right mind would be paranoid knowing the time he could get for this shit. On the flip side, knowing that a nigga out here is hungry like I am will lay a nigga down for this.

I was scanning the area looking up the street and then down the street around the carwash. There was no one in sight other than Ace, D.C., and his bitch, so I pulled the bag out of the trunk and made my way over to this nigga who was gripping the bag of money.

As I was extending the bag out for D.C. to grab, I heard the screeching of tires that seemed to come from out of nowhere. I turned quick only to see that it was a Ford Crown Victoria coming into the carwash, and fast. The only thing I could think of was that I had to get the fuck outta there.

I turned quickly and ran back to my whip. In the midst of me sprinting back to my Benz, a voice boomed through the air.

"Get down! Freeze! You're under arrest!"

They had me. My reign at the top was over. This

wasn't the local police or state troopers. It was them boys at the FBI. They blocked in my whip, knowing they didn't want to risk me taking them on a high-speed chase.

I turned around to face the commanding voice, only to see that it was this nigga D.C. and the white bitch pointing guns at me. For a split second it felt like a bad dream. This nigga right here is with them, I thought.

I'm still strapped with my Glock 40 on my waistline, thinking about laying this nigga out, even with the odds of being killed right here on the spot. That's the level of betrayal I was feeling right now. The nigga that introduced me to D.C. was dead once I sent word out. It was simply a matter of time.

As he approached me, the bitch he was with had this look of happiness on her face. As for this nigga, he was smiling, which pissed me off even more.

"I got you, Tommy Guns. You're under arrest."

"Fuck you, you stupid muthafucka!"

The agents moved in and began to pat me down until Ace snapped up and unexpectedly fired off his MAC-11. The burst of slugs raced through the air violently, crashing into D.C. and the white bitch he was with.

She fell with a head shot. D.C. was hit in the leg and shoulder, which spun him, only to be hit from the side and puncture one of his lungs before dropping him beside his partner.

The agents handling me immediately took cover, not expecting what was happening. Shit, I dropped down so my little cousin could handle his business.

Big Ivan came just in time, seeing this shit unfold as it was. He didn't hesitate to join the chaos, especially seeing Ace being fired on by the agents.

He grabbed his riot pump out of the back seat before jumping out and placing the agents in the middle. At the same time, he caught them by surprise. Another problem they weren't expecting.

I was looking at this nigga D.C. on the ground barely breathing. He was looking at me, too, but this nigga was smiling now. A sadistic smirk came across my face seeing the fear in this nigga's eyes. He was scared of dying. That's the difference between him and me. I know this shit comes with the territory.

I was pinned down by the gunfire from Ace and the Federal agents trying to keep him at bay. I started reaching discreetly for my Glock, obviously wanting to help my fam.

Big Ivan downed two agents with the brute force of the riot pump.

It was blood in and blood out with my cousins. They wouldn't let me down, and I wasn't going to let them down either.

The agents moved in, using tactical procedures to close in on Ace, while the other agents were radioing in for backup upon seeing that Big Ivan had them pinned down.

Ace dumped the whole thirty-three rounds before popping the clip out and flipping it around to the other clip that was duct taped to it, which allowed him to have a fast reload.

That shifted their attention from me, which was the third mistake they made today. I got up quick and closed my trunk with the bricks in it. I didn't want to leave my cousins; besides, I wanted to get this bitch-ass nigga, D.C.

I first walked up and stood over the undercover female bitch, and then fired one off into her skull just to make sure she was dead. Then I squatted down to the barely breathing-ass nigga.

"You a stupid muthafucka! Thinking you can

infiltrate me and my network. You thought shit was funny. How you feel now, nigga?"

I didn't even give him a chance to plead his way out or infiltrate anyone else's organization. I squeezed off a slug into the eyes that were staring back at me. Then I spit on the nigga as I stood up.

The sound of my gunfire alerted the other agents, who reacted fast, firing off and catching me with slugs. They were accurate, but they didn't want me dead. They wanted me alive to stand trial.

Sirens could be heard approaching quickly. The Harrisburg police were coming fast. Helicopters were also approaching. It was probably the news crews.

Officers arrived shortly and forced Big Ivan to the ground, shooting him in the back. He was still trying to move and get off one more shot at the cop that shot him in the back. But they swarmed him fast and kicked the gun away.

Ace was still sending bursts of gunfire from his position, killing one of the Federal agents with an unforgiving headshot. That alone raised the level of fury for the agents as they moved in and cornered Ace.

"It ain't sweet! Y'all think this shit is sweet? Let my cousin go, and I'll let some of y'all live!" Ace yelled out, ready to die while holding me down.

He didn't see Big Ivan drop. I did, which made me reach for the Glock that was thrown from my hand when they shot me. But they rushed in and shut that idea down.

I was feeling fucked up because I didn't want Ace to go all out because they had us; and with all the backup that came and with the helicopters in the sky, we weren't going to get away. An ambulance also came fast to tend to the wounded officers and Federal agents first. Me and Big Ivan were the last of their worries. Even though they wanted us alive, they knew our wounds weren't life-threatening.

~ ~ ~

Ace's cell phone sounded off and vibrated at the same time. This crazy little nigga took the call, seeing that it was from one of his bitches. He had his back up against the wall squatted down so his whip could protect him from oncoming gunfire.

"Candy! Candy! Shit is crazy right now. I'm not going make it tonight, baby girl."

She already knew what was going on because the

news choppers were showing everything live feed from the air.

"I can see y'all on the news right now. Don't do anything stupid or get hurt."

"I'm way past that point right now!" Ace said as he raised his gun up to fire again after hearing the agents moving in close.

The gunfire was loud coming through the cell phone and scared Candy even more. She was his ride-or-die white bitch. She also ran an escort service, so she had hoes too, and her own paper, but she loved my little cuz.

"Give yourself up, baby. You can't win, especially from what I'm looking at. They're closing in on you from every angle."

Hearing this made him alert. Knowing they were closing in, he dropped the cell phone and jumped to his feet, turning the corner fast with gun in his hand and finger on the trigger. He was ready to squeeze, but no one was there. They were still behind the other corner, but the agents coming from the other direction were now behind Ace.

"Drop the weapon and get down!" they all sounded off.

Their level of adrenaline was running high. A split second was all it took to change the course of this attempted arrest.

Knowing Ace, he would try these muthafuckas. I couldn't blame him. It beat rotting in a cell for the rest of your life.

He turned looking over his shoulder to see how many agents were there. There were five of them, with five guns aimed at him. He squatted down and placed the gun on the ground. Then he placed his hands behind his head and interlocked them.

The agents moved in fast, securing him and the weapon. Shit was crazy. It wasn't supposed to happen like this, with all three of us at the same time.

~ ~ ~

Fox News was reporting live, showing the footage of me and my cousins being tended to by the medics while they gave their views on what took place and what they had learned thus far.

"Tom 'Tommy Guns' Anderson, along with his cousins, held these officers and Federal agents at bay with gunfire until moments ago. A few agents have been murdered in this crossfire as well as a few wounded. This all derived from a drug arrest that went terribly wrong. Mr. Anderson is believed to be responsible for over 80 percent of the cocaine distribution throughout the central Pennsylvania area. A drug mastermind that has been undetected until his organization was infiltrated by one of the FBI's own."

The news reporter ran her mouth off on what she thought was going on. However, on the other side of the city, close to the suburbs, Rakman Hussein, a member of the Muslim Brotherhood, also a man known for terrorist acts of violence around the world, was watching the news. He was also the one driving the Bentley Flying Spur.

The six foot, 190-pound Saudi Arabian-born killer was only forty, and wore his facial hair closely trimmed with razor perfection. His appearance was very business-looking, with his black hair cut close on the sides and flowing with his facial hair.

He recognized my face on the news from seeing me at the Giants as well as at the warehouse when I was handling business with D.C.

He now had a name with the face. More importantly, he knew where I was going. He also knew that I was into getting this money.

He called up his cousin, Amir Hussein, the one that who was driving the Mercedes 65 Brabus. He picked up on the first ring, because he too, was watching the news and was preparing to call Rakman.

His Saudi accent was strong, but he spoke smoothly and calmly.

"This American from the warehouse is all over the news. Federal agents are everywhere. This is not a coincidence that we see him on the news—and twice in the same day as we did. These Americans cannot be trusted as you can be. We must have everything as planned. No flaws," Rakman said.

Rakman and Amir were sleeper cells. Although Rakman was high ranking and rich, there was someone above him pulling the strings.

"I will take care of this as soon as possible. Everything will go as planned. Allah knows best. *Allah u Akbar.*"

"*Allah u Akbar. As-salamu alaykum.*"

"May peace be unto you, Rakman."

CHAPTER 11

A FEW DAYS PASSED by and King Jose of New York was wondering what the fuck was going on with Tommy Guns. He normally would have called or come to the city by now. Due to the fact that he didn't trust many, he started thinking that Tommy was either dead or in jail. Either way, he wanted his money from the fifty bricks of raw he fronted him, which was a total of $750,000.

"This *maricon no llamame en tres hoy!*" King Jose snapped, thinking about his money. "It's always something with them *morenos!*" he continued. "*Oye esta ahora!* We go to see this *punta* in his city!" he said to the team of Latino goons, who were all ready to kill to show their loyalty and respect.

As King Jose was preparing his team to make a move, down in Florida, the infamous Turnpike Tito was racing down the highway in his CL65 AMG Mercedes Benz with the top down to display the all-white interior.

He was loving the four-lane highway as he opened up, doing a little over 100 MPH while getting head from this sexy-ass, light-brown-skinned chick favoring a young Halle, with a tight workout body that allowed her jeans to hug every curve. Her head was going up and down smoothly, working her magic as he mashed the gas and speed-dialed Tommy Guns at the same time.

No answer. He called back, this time getting a busy signal. At first he didn't think anything of it, but his instinct kicked in. This time he called Big Ivan's phone. No answer. Busy signal. His mind started racing as the only thoughts came to mind. These *morenos* is dead or in jail.

"Mami, stop!" he said to her since he was no longer in the mood.

At the same time, he raced to the side of the highway, coming to an abrupt stop. He then jumped out of the car and dialed both of their numbers again, only to get the same signal that only meant bad news.

"*Cono! Ahi Dios mio!* This is not happening!" he snapped, pacing back and forth. "They don't want this type of war! I'll kill all of those puntas!" he said while staring at the screen of his phone as if he was dialing the wrong numbers, but he wasn't, and he knew at that moment something needed to be done.

"If he don't have my money, then he has earned death!" he said.

He then became silent as thoughts were racing through his mind. He then made the much-needed phone call to all his associates below and above him, so they would know his next move. He jumped back into his car, allowing the sexy morena to work her lips again, and she did just that, bringing him some satisfaction after feeling the rage of anger streaming through his body.

CHAPTER 12

THEY GOT ME AT the fucked-up Dauphin County Prison in Harrisburg where the food is scraps, the conditions are shitty, and the guards need a bullet face-first. The nurses, on the other hand, have been looking out for me since I've been in the medical department healing from my bullet wounds. That shootout shit was crazy and had my adrenaline flowing, but it's the life I chose and the life many of us live. This is our end game when it comes down to it. The crazy shit is that my cousins fell with me. I need them to be on the outside, since I owe all this bread out. These Spanish niggas are about the paper, so I got to get word to them, because I don't want them to think that I'm on some bullshit.

As my thoughts were flowing and I was thinking about what I needed done, I heard my gate unlock. So, I got up and made my way over to the door.

"What the fuck do these idiots want?" I was thinking as I saw the captain and two guards approaching my cell.

"Turn around and put your hands behind your

back, inmate," the guard demanded.

I didn't resist, especially knowing my condition. Whatever it is they wanted wasn't normal procedure.

"Take a seat on your bunk, inmate," the guard continued with an attitude like I did something to him or his family.

I did just that. I sat down. When the two guards exited the cell, the captain came in.

"I'm Captain Mohamad," he said introducing himself.

The first thing that came to my mind was that he was with them Arab muthafuckas that I saw at the Giants. Little did I know, he was the real-deal sleeper cell as a member of the Muslim Brotherhood. Realizing his possible association with these Arab niggas, I didn't take my eyes off him.

"Mr. Anderson, I hear we have some problems."

Before I could respond, this muthafucka put his hand on my bullet wound and placed pressure on it. The pain shot through my body. I was trying to cuss this muthafucka out, but he put his hand over my mouth.

"If you say anything to the Feds about what you seen or think you saw, then this pain you're feeling will be the least of your worries. You won't leave here alive," he threatened me with a sadistic smirk across his face.

Little does he know, if I wasn't injured or handcuffed, I would have been kicking his ass right now.

"I don't know what the fuck you're talking about!" I said, giving him a dark stare and allowing him to know that I didn't back down from any man that bled like me.

But it made me think back to these muthafuckas shooting at me and my fam. It was crazy shit. These Arab niggas were more paranoid than me. He was looking at me shaking his head in disbelief as if I really knew what the fuck they were into.

"You'll be sorry, my friend. I tell you this. Maybe your cousins will say different of what they know."

"Leave my folks out of this. Like I said, I don't know shit, and they don't either!" I said as he turned away, ignoring me as if I wasn't there.

The guards came back in and aggressively removed the cuffs before exiting the cell, leaving me to my thoughts on what just took place, as if I didn't have enough to deal with.

CHAPTER 13

ON THE OTHER SIDE of the city, King Jose was coming through with his team of goons following behind his CLS 600 Mercedes Benz. His team was in four separate H2 Hummers that were all black with tinted windows concealing the murderous rage in all of their eyes. They were twenty deep and all in pursuit of tracking down Tommy Guns, fully armed, and ready to take care of business.

King Jose knew where Tommy Guns hung out because he had come to the city before to party with Tommy.

"Oye, he hangs out a few blocks from here. Go that way!" King Jose said as they turned off of Cameron Street going over the Maclay Street bridge toward Green Street, also known as Duck-Down Avenue. The street was nicknamed due to the many shootouts and drive-bys. King Jose called his goons in the trucks to make them aware of what this city was about and not to underestimate this city. King Jose saw a group of hustlas out and about, so he decided this was where he'd have his driver stop.

"Oye, pull over right there."

As his gold Benz came to a stop, the H2 Hummers followed. All came to a halt before they all stepped out fully strapped with ARs and Tek-9s ready for whatever. Once his goons secured the area, he stepped out and looked around before walking up to Tommy's mom's crib and knocking on the door. The little niggas in the hood were looking on at them knowing whose crib that was: Tommy Guns'. As he waited on a response to his knock on the door, the young hustlers started approaching wondering what was going on. At the same time, they wanted to know who these Spanish niggas were.

Not getting an answer at the door made him even more upset, since he was thinking about his money and getting paid.

"Mira, kick that shit in!" he said while pointing at the door.

As soon as the door swung open, the men entered looking for Tommy Guns or anything that would tell them where he was. King Jose entered behind his men, only to see the mail on the floor. What stood out to him was a letter with the correctional jail stamp with Tommy's name on it. Right then he knew he wasn't taken for his money, but now he wanted to know how he was going to get paid. Because that type of bread wasn't going to be unpaid no matter what happened to Tommy.

Just as he was reading the letter, he could hear the young teens outside of the house yelling, "Yo, what the fuck are y'all doing up in that old lady's crib?"

They knew whose house it belonged to, and they all had respect for the old head.

"*Yo quiero, mi chabo!* That's what the fuck I'm doing here!" he said, turning to face the young goons, only to see that they were strapped and ready to go.

At that same moment, King Jose's goons saw this and shielded him as gunshots rang out.

"*Vamos! Vamos!* Get King Jose to the car!" the Spanish thug yelled out as they raced him to the car while ducking the barrage of gunfire.

At the same time, they returned by unloading their fully automatic weapons that roared through the air as slugs slammed into the cars around as well as the young thugs trying to defend their turf. One of the young teens hit the ground as slugs slammed into his chest and arm. He didn't give up. His adrenaline was rushing through his body as he raised his pistol and continued firing off shots to assist his homies. Shit was getting heated as sirens could be heard in the background.

"*Oye vamos policia!*" Jose's goon yelled out, mashing the gas and getting away with ease in the Benz.

The young bucks all rushed over to their downed homie and picked him up.

"You good? We got to get out of here. They coming. I could hear them," the oldest teen said. "Go through the alleyway. My whip is back there in the parking lot."

As they made their way through the side of the houses, the cops came with fast tires screeching in each direction, but they were gone, making their way to get their homie medical attention. At the same time, they were feeling good about holding down their big homie, Tommy Guns, even without his knowledge or consent.

CHAPTER 14

THE NEXT DAY AT the warehouse on Industrial Road, Amir and Rakman were inside overlooking their men loading up four different cargo vans with dynamite and C-4 explosives.

"We're on the right track with everything going as we planned it to get America's attention. This is going to be bigger than the last one we set, which crippled this country," Rakman said.

"*Allah u Akbar.*"

"Yes, he is, Amir," Rakman said. He then added, "Did you secure that situation with that black drug dealer the Feds picked up?"

"Yes, but I don't believe that he knows anything based on what has taken place with him and his cousins. He is a simple drug dealer."

"Take care of it!" Rakman said, abruptly cutting off his cousin. "There is a lot at stake, and we cannot afford to allow something like this simple drug dealer, as you say, sidetrack what we've planned. Many powerful people are expecting us to fulfill this mission, and I will not fail!" Rakman said with his arms folded. *"Allah u Akbar."*

Amir respected and feared his cousin, so getting things done meant taking care of all loose ends.

Amir was only twenty-nine years old and stood a firm five foot ten and weighed 175 pounds. He had a closely shaven beard groomed along with his close haircut. He too was a member of the Muslim Brotherhood as well as a follower of his cousin, standing firm in his beliefs to wake America up. To him, death is a privilege if he becomes a martyr in the name of Allah.

The Arab men were loading up enough explosives to level half of the city. This many explosives would get America's attention and many more countries' too.

As Amir exited the warehouse to take care of the business at hand with Tommy Guns and his cousins, Rakman began directing the team of Arab goons to their locations.

"Men, you all know what to do, as we have planned this for some time. Now get in your positions. Talib, you and your crew go to the governor's mansion. Habeeb, you take your team to Three Mile Island (TMI). The last two vans will position yourselves at the capitol building, and make sure you two teams wear the uniforms provided. May Allah be with you all."

"Allah u Akbar!" all the men chimed while exiting the warehouse ready to do their deed of becoming martyrs in the name of Allah. They sought the virgins in the afterlife as well as other things they believed would come to them upon their suicide missions in the name of Allah.

These Arab men were all brainwashed in their twenties by their mentors and what they believed to be true.

It didn't take long before the men arrived at the capitol building in their uniforms, looking like maintenance men pushing dollies with C-4 plastic explosives and dynamite concealed throughout in light bulbs and toolboxes. They entered without any resistance or confrontation. They made their way through the capitol, placing the explosives in the bathroom vents, ceiling, trashcans, etc. Once they secured the explosives in their locations, the men began heading back to their vans, but not before a capitol police officer's voice boomed through the air getting their attention while at the same time placing them on high alert.

"Hey, you guys! Hey, stop!"

At that very moment, each of the men closed their eyes trying to bring calm over themselves. They then opened their eyes as each of them leaned down to their toolboxes to get their Glock 9mms. They were ready to kill and die right then and there if the cop didn't say or do the right thing by them.

The cop came up fast breathing a little heavy.

"Is that your guys' vans out by the fountain?" he asked, allowing the moment of fire and adrenaline to come to a calm.

"Yes sir, those are our vans. We are going to move them now. We just came from repairing a few things."

"Good, because we can't be having anything blocking the fountains," the officer said, not realizing his closeness to death in dealing with these suicidal maniacs.

As the men were making their way out toward the exit, the officer yelled out again, "Hey, guys!"

In this very moment, they all were ready to go, no second-guessing what he wanted. It was kill him time and then detonate all the bombs.

"Don't forget to sign the book on the way out," the officer said, reminding them at the same time yet spiking their level of adrenaline. The Arab men smirked, thinking about how the officer was about to get his clock punched early if he would have said or done something else.

Once outside they called up Rakman.

"My brother, it is done."

"Allah u Akbar, and may He be with you in your last moments," Rakman said, knowing his men would carry this out until the end.

"*Allah u Akbar*! I'll see you in paradise after we complete stage two of this journey."

"I'll greet you with open arms," Rakman said, before hanging up the phone and thinking about how it was all coming together.

CHAPTER 15

TURNPIKE TITO AND HIS team of Latino goons were all just rolling in, getting off at the I-83 bridge. They were ready to track down Tommy Guns to get paid their money. Turnpike Tito was rolling in style in his new sky-blue Bentley GT coupe with a white leather interior, chrome 22s, and a sound system all to his likings. Tito's goons were all on custom Hiabusa 1300ccs outfitted with compartments to conceal their fully automatic 9mm Uzis. Twenty goons on bikes followed behind Tito as he mashed the gas, gliding over the bridge and making his way off the ramp into the Downtown area where all of the restaurants and nightclubs were located.

As he drove down the street with the motorcycles roaring behind him, he made a call to Big Ivan's phone. There was no answer, so he called Tommy's number. No answer. This only added fuel to the fire. He made his way uptown driving past a lot of people before he noticed a bar on 6th Street called Roebucks. It was a little after 9:00 p.m., and the traffic to the club was picking up inside and out.

Turnpike Tito noticed this, so he made an abrupt U-turn. His goons did the same, revving their engines and rumbling the streets, which was getting everyone's attention within earshot. He came to a stop across from the bar and double-parked his whip. He hopped out, while his goons followed when they saw their boss crossing the street.

"I'm looking for Big Ivan and Tommy Guns," he said, looking at the crowd that was standing around drinking out of plastic cups, some smoking weed or rolling up blunts.

They were all looking back at him like he was crazy coming up asking for two hood legends like he was the cops or something. They knew he wasn't the cops, but niggas in the hood don't just volunteer people's whereabouts. It's the code of the streets. He knew this, so he decided to add a little more incentive to make them talk.

"I got three stacks right here if somebody tells me where I can find them."

"I need that money. My baby needs clothes, and I need to turn up tonight. What you really want to know?" this brown-skinned sista said, who stood five foot even with a blonde wig, green contacts, tight jeans, and a cut-off T-shirt pressing against her breasts to show off her perfect nipples.

Tito smiled briefly seeing her push her way through the crowd, only to greet him with a smile and her hand out.

"Give me the money, and I got you."

He handed the money over to her. He knew that neither she nor anyone out there would be able to go anywhere as long as his goons were standing by ready to put in work.

"Them fools is at the county jail at 501 Mall Road. They was shooting out with the FBI," she said, taking her fingers through the stack of money and fanning it out.

He was looking on at her pissed about what he was hearing, so he snatched the money from her and turned, walking away. All of her happy hopes dissipated when it was taken away.

"What the fuck is wrong with you taking the money you said I could have it in exchange for where they at?"

"Your information is useless to me," he said, walking back to his car.

She wanted that money badly, so she wanted to run behind him and claw his ass up, but she knew the

Spanish goons he was with wouldn't allow that to happen.

"I can get you in contact with him," she yelled out to him, now getting his attention again. "My sister is a guard at the prison."

She made her way over to the car where he was. She knew that he was interested.

"What's your name, mami?"

"Jasmine Davis."

"You get me in contact with him, and you will be rewarded. Take this money to give you a little motivation and know that there is plenty more where that came from if you do the right thing," he said as he gave her his number.

"What's your name, pretty boy?"

"*Llámame* Tito. My name is Tito," he said, turning to get into his car.

He then mashed the gas and headed to the Downtown area to party. Lucky for him it was Latin night at the Dragonfly nightclub. Turnpike Tito was now feeling a little better about where his associate Tommy Guns was. He knew he didn't get burnt for his money. Now he just had to figure out where the money or product was.

CHAPTER 16

BACK OUT AT THE prison, I was lying up in my cell chilling and thinking about the shit this nigga King Jose did at my mom's spot. Truth be told, that nigga would be dead if I got close to him after he kicked in my mom's door like he had lost his fucking mind. At the same time, he didn't even show any type of respect for me or my gangsta. So, he was officially burnt for his bread and all. I had that shit in the tuck. I had to send word to my cousins to let them know what was good in case this nigga Jose tried to send somebody at them through one of those gangs and shit, like MS13, Latin Kings, or Los Zetas. All them crazy-ass niggas that were about they work no matter what the deal was as long as they got paid for getting it done.

"Anderson," a voice called my name, bringing me back to the reality of this hell hole.

I looked over at the door and saw a female sergeant standing there. Good thing it wasn't that Arab captain that came through.

"What's good?" I said, getting up to make my

way over to the door. "I got a message from this nigga named Tito. He's in town and wanted to know where you were."

"How did you get this message?" I asked, being a little paranoid.

"My cousin, Jasmine, from Uptown, said he came through. He was deep with a team looking serious in search of you and your folks, Big Ivan and Ace."

Damn, this shit was crazy! These niggas both came looking for me like I was the type that burns people. I wasn't into that. I was a money chaser.

"He knows why you're here," she added while I was processing my thoughts.

"I owe Jasmine with the fat ass and pretty eyes?" I said, which made her laugh a little. "Yeah, that's her."

"Let him know that I got that, and I'll try to figure out how to get it to him. It would be nice if you had a phone to let me call him direct," I said, checking her temp to see if she would really let me get away with that. "I doubt that, my man. I did you a favor with this."

"I appreciate you for real. I had to see if you

would do more," I said while she smiled it off.

"I did see your name on the transfer list to Cumberland County. I take it you're high risk. You and your cousins all are. They got them going somewhere else."

"This shit is crazy. What the fuck is they doing that for?" I said, venting. I knew she wouldn't be able to do anything about it anyway. "Let Tito know about this transfer. Soon as I can, I'll get someone to make a move to get him his money and investments," I said, meaning the rest of the cocaine.

"I got you. Stay focused and get healthy with your bullet wound and all. I'll tell my cousin you remember her from her fat ass, too," she said before walking away and leaving me to think about all of this shit that was going on with my life.

CHAPTER 17

BACK OVER AT THE Dragonfly nightclub, Turnpike Tito was enjoying himself and loving the women of this city. He was in the VIP section popping bottles with all of the women living the good life. His cell phone sounded off. He didn't hear it, but he could see the light flashing on the table in front of him, so he leaned forward and recognized the 717-area code. It could only be one person, he figured, since Tommy was in jail; and the only other person to have his number now was Jasmine. He grabbed the phone and made his way toward the staircase, where the music wasn't as loud, and you could hear the person on the other end of the phone. His security followed without being told. They knew the drill of protecting a boss of his status.

"Jasmine, tell me something good," he said while answering the phone.

"I got some good news, pretty boy, but not over the phone."

"I'll be at the Crown Plaza in a few minutes. When you get to the lobby, call me again and I'll give you the suite number," he responded, being cautious not being from this city, and also knowing that he needed his men to be on point for her coming alone.

"I'm on my way, pretty boy," she said before hanging up.

Turnpike Tito went back to the VIP section where the beautiful women were.

"Ladies, the party for me is over here, but you two can come and continue the party at my hotel suite," he said, pointing out two sexy-ass Latinas looking like telenovela models.

They exited the club and jumped into his whip with the top down, flexing on everyone looking on.

"Ahi, papi, you killing them with this baby and white leather," the blonde Latina said.

"I know that shit is so soft it's like massaging *mi culo*, papi," the dark-haired Latina said while rubbing her ass up and down on the plush leather.

He just smiled knowing this was the life.

It didn't take long to get to the hotel. Tito and the women were all in his suite while the goons were on the other side of the suite by the entrance giving the boss his space. Tito popped open a few bottles, giving them what they wanted and more. The blonde

Latina was filling out her tight blue jeans, with a silk top flowing over her 36C sized breasts. Her nails were done, her lips were on point, and her eyes glowed green. The other Latina favored her friend. The only difference was she was wearing black jeans, and a silver top that enhanced her gray eyes.

The alcohol led to kisses, and the kisses led to them making their way over to the couch and undressing each other with heavy touching and caressing, stimulating one another with each passing touch. Moans filled the air as these two Latinas started roaming their hands over one another. They started kissing each other in between kissing on his neck while pulling off his pants. He liked every bit of this. The dark-haired Latina took her soft hands and slid them down into his silk boxer shorts and pumped it to make him more erect with each stroke.

"I like this, mami. Put it in your mouth," he ordered.

She did just that as the other Latina started to finger her girlfriend, who moaned out loud.

"Ahi, ahi, I like this shit! Mmmmmmh!"

Her humming sound vibrated over his dick and made him feel good while she was getting fingered.

Just as things were heating up, his cell phone sounded off and got his attention. Most men would continue on with these two beautiful women in their presence, but not Turnpike Tito. He knew this was a business call.

"Stop *espera un minute*," he said, walking over to his phone. It was Jasmine. "Jasmine, talk to me."

"I'm here in the lobby."

"I'm staying in suite 708," he said, looking over at the Latinas who were now pleasing each other with fingers and tongues, both moaning in satisfaction.

He hung up the phone and made his way back over to join them. Jasmine made her way up to the suite. Before knocking on the door, she fixed herself to look good and presentable for this out-of-town boss. She also checked the message her cousin sent her so she would be able to say the right thing. She knocked on the door, ready to deliver the message and get the reward he had promised. Although, she was looking for the prize in him.

Tito came to the door with his hotel robe on and welcomed her inside.

"Somebody is ready for the night," he said, noticing that she had changed into something sexier than before.

She had on red jeans that fit her tight body, light brown suede Dolce & Gabbana six-inch pumps, and a handbag to match. Her white silk top was open just enough to show her cleavage.

"I wanted to look the part, as a boss chick coming to see a boss man," she replied, eyeing him up and down as she made her way into the room. She immediately could hear the voices of females, which shifted her intentions. Then she saw them as she made her way into the room. "Hmmmm, I thought you were strictly business, but I see you got sidetracked," she said sarcastically.

"I'm always business. Those two don't account for anything. If they did, you would still be in the lobby waiting on me to answer the phone," he responded, shifting his tone as well as her thoughts of him. "Now, what good news do you have for me?"

"Tommy said he's going to figure out a way to get you your money and product. But more importantly, they are transferring him to another jail tomorrow. He'll be at Cumberland County prison across the river."

Turnpike Tito was feeling a step closer to

securing his money but was concerned about this transfer. This was something he would have his men look into.

"Thank you for your time and information. Would you care to stay and have a drink with me?" he asked, making his way over to the minibar.

"I could do a drink; besides, I deserve it, right? Plus, you still have to give me my reward," she added with a smirk.

He grabbed a stack of money he had on the bar and slid it over to her along with a double shot of Patron Silver.

"To the good life, knowing that the sky is the limit," he said, raising his glass to toast with her. They both drank the shots fast, before he then leaned over to kiss Jasmine on the cheek. "Thank you again, beautiful. Make sure you keep me updated with Tommy if anything changes."

"I will," she said, picking up her money and placing it into her bag as she glanced over at the Latinas still going at it. Tito noticed her roaming eyes.

"Would you like to join the party?" he asked as he poured another shot for the two of them.

"You sexy as hell, but I don't do chicks. I like the dick too much. So, call me when you got some alone time," she responded before slamming her shot and turning to exit the suite.

This allowed him to look on at her sexy fat ass while she was working her magic through them jeans. She knew he was watching, so she veered over her shoulder with a smile and said, "*Tu gusta*, pretty boy?"

He shook his head yes. At the same time, he knew she was full of fun. There was something different about her and not routine as the chicks he had over there on the couch.

"*Buenos noches, bonita*," he said as she exited the room.

He then made his way back over to the Latinas on the couch. Sex wasn't his real focus. Tommy Guns and his money was, but the women would pass the night.

CHAPTER 18

AT 8:00 A.M. THE next day, Amir dialed his associate, Captain Mohammad, to check up on Tommy Guns. He wanted to know what he knew, if anything at all. He also wanted to erase him and his cousins, just to be on the safe side of things.

"*As-salamu alaykum,* my brother," Captain Mohamad said, already knowing who was on the other end of the phone.

"*Walaikum assalam.* Have you taken care of the problem?" Amir asked, getting straight to the point.

"I confronted them all, but nothing."

"Don't be foolish. They crossed our paths twice. Just take care of it. Rakman will be calling you soon."

Captain Mohamad was now feeling compromised knowing that he needed to take care of this business, or he and his family would pay.

"Has anyone come to see him, or has he made any calls that would be alarming?" Amir questioned, wanting to know more.

"No one has come to visit him. As for the calls,

we monitor them, and there has been nothing strange." There was a pause before he added, "I did see his name on a morning transfer, so he will be leaving this prison. The FBI is separating him and his cousins."

Hearing this information made Amir want to expedite things even more.

"Take care of it as I said before."

"It will be done," he responded.

Amir hung up the phone, leaving Mohamad to deal with the problem that he thought Tommy Guns and his cousins were becoming.

At 8:22 a.m. King Jose was at the Hilton Hotel waiting on a call about Tommy Guns. He too passed out some money to get info on him.

Jay Jay from Uptown called King Jose.

"*Hola, que tal, mi amigo?*" Jose answered the phone upon seeing that it was a local number. "Ya boy is getting transferred around 11:00 this morning; maybe sooner. Just be on point."

"*Gracias, amigo.* Good doing business with you." Jose hung up the phone and turned to his goons in the room. "*Mira esta ahora.* That punta is leaving the jail, so we got to go see what's going on."

He knew his team needed to be all the way on point, especially with Federal transfers, since they were real slick with them.

Back over at the Crown Plaza, Turnpike Tito, along with his men, was already on point knowing the Feds would be keeping a tight lid on the security with this transit. So, he figured the best spot would be in the parking lot across from the prison, which was also the Harrisburg East Mall.

At 9:00 a.m. Rakman was on the phone calling his cousin, Amir.

"As-salamu alaykum."

"Walaikum assalam," Amir responded. "I am in position awaiting the transfer," he said while sitting close to the mall to keep an eye on when they exited the prison's grounds.

"Are they moving all three at once?"

"Mohamad took care of one, I know for sure, serving him a bad breakfast," Amir said, referring to Big Ivan's cyanide-laced scrambled eggs. The kitchen and its inmates would take the blame for this.

"And the other two?"

"I'll call him when we hang up."

"I'm hanging up now. Don't fail me or this

cause."

Rakman didn't care about who was in the way or involved. Everyone who he felt was a threat to succeed in getting America's attention would die.

Amir was looking over at the prison and checking the movement to see what was going on, before calling Mohamad.

"Hello!" Mohamad said, answering his phone as if he was dreading the call.

"My brother, have you made any other progress?"

"Yes, yes! The little one took his own life hanging up this morning."

"Allah u Akbar. We will finish the rest from here. I'll see you in paradise, brother," Amir said, hanging up the phone while now patiently waiting to take care of the loose ends.

At 9:15 a.m. King Jose and his team were casing out the prison, knowing that the Feds were going to be securing the transfer since this was a high-profile case. His men were also aware that this wasn't going to be easy, so being smart in this situation was going to be vital. The good thing they had on their side was the element of surprise. No one would expect them to come fast and fully loaded to jack a transit to get Tommy Guns.

~ ~ ~

Back inside of the prison, I was sitting in my cell wiping away the tears that I had shed for my cousins, knowing it was no accident or by-chance death. This was more like a hit from some organized muthafuckas.

I have to be on point now because they are coming for me next. They got both of my cousins. Maybe it was the Feds for what we did to them, or them Arab niggas thinking we saw something they were doing. Either way, I can't go out like that. I knew if I figured out who did this, they would pay in blood.

~ ~ ~

Turnpike Tito got info at 9:50 that morning on a secure route the Feds planned on using to move Tommy Guns. He also found out that both of Tommy's cousins were dead. That itself raised suspicions, making him think about what and who was behind it. Jasmine then texted Tito the route that was given to her by her cousin. It was a detailed text outlining the primary and secondary routes. Tito was very appreciative of this, so he sent her a text back that read: Maybe soon we'll do a weekend in Miami and get lost in my mansion.

She loved the thought as she sent a text back: Mmmmmmmmm (followed by smiley faces).

~ ~ ~

By 10:00 a.m., four black unmarked Suburbans approached the Dauphin County Prison boasting four agents in each vehicle concealed behind the dark tinted windows. They all pulled up in single file and back-to-back, before coming to a halt once the gates closed behind them. The agents in the second truck all jumped out and headed into the prison while the other agents stood by manning their radios and doing a weapons check.

Tommy Guns' case was now national news. It was also widespread news that his cousins suddenly died in one way or another. Without question, the Feds would be looking into that, but for now, they were present to secure Tommy Guns.

The agents didn't take long once inside the prison. They flashed their credentials. There was no small talk. It was now game time. The guards already had Tommy in the holding cell waiting for this moment.

~ ~ ~

"Tom Anderson, you're a popular person today," the agent said, seeing me come through the door. "We're going to secure you with this vest as standard protocol. Then I'm going to need you to face this way to be cuffed, and then we'll be on our way."

"Why am I being transferred?" I asked.

"We're doing a job. We don't ask questions. Besides, your cousins didn't seem to settle in with the conditions of this prison," the agent said.

I gave him a dark stare. What he said made me think, but at the same time, I was pissed.

"Heading out, one in tow," the agent said, radioing to the vehicles in the sally port.

~ ~ ~

They made their way out to the trucks and loaded up Tommy. Each of the vehicles then lined up behind one another. This tactic was also to deceive anyone looking on, so they would not be able to pinpoint the Suburban in which the high-profile inmate was placed. It didn't matter that King Jose and his team were rolling out discreetly behind the convoy. Amir was also following close by because he too needed to fulfill his orders from Rakman. It was a must that this would be taken care of.

The convoy drove through the city down Paxton Street, heading toward the 17th Street exit that would merge to the I-83 highway. All of the agents were on full alert, with weapons loaded, eyes open, and radio frequencies open for communication. Each agent in the front seat checked the rear-view mirrors as well as the side mirrors.

All of the agents carried Glock 9mms and a few extra clips as well as AR-15s for high-risk situations such as this. As the convoy was merging onto the highway, Tommy Guns started seeing a gang of custom motorcycles followed by a custom sky-blue Bentley coupe. As the trucks passed by, Tommy looked into the Bentley and saw Turnpike Tito. The strange thing was that Tito was looking back as if he could see through the dark tinted windows, or as if he knew what vehicle he was in.

Once the trucks all passed by, Tommy was still looking behind him and could see what was about to happen, because he knew Tito didn't position himself for nothing.

"Hey, did you lose something back there or

what?" the agent asked Tommy, upon seeing that he was focused on what was behind them.

The agents also saw the bikes and car, since it was their job to pay attention to things like that.

Tommy gave the agent a look before he was ready to respond. Suddenly, a burst of gunfire slammed into the lead truck.

"Incoming fire! Code 3!" the agent yelled over the radio as slugs sounded off and hit the truck.

The driver swerved while trying to evade the oncoming slugs as other agents positioned themselves to return fire.

Tommy also shifted his focus in the direction of the bullets and saw they were coming from the H2 Hummers racing across the six-lane bridge. The lead Federal vehicle fired off precise rounds into the first H2 Hummer causing them to swerve and crash. The Federal convoy continued on racing down the highway as bullets came nonstop.

"Are these your fucking friends, Anderson?" the agent yelled out at Tommy Guns.

"I don't have any friends, only family," he responded as his attention went toward the gold CLS600 pulling up to the side truck he was in.

It was King Jose with a 9mm Uzi in his hand.

"Oh shit!" Tommy yelled out, ducking down just as a slew of automatic gunfire tore through the truck and its windows.

"Ram to your right!" the agent yelled out.

"What the hell you say?"

"Ram! Ram to your right!"

With the level of adrenaline flowing with the roaring of gunfire, it was almost hard to hear or concentrate. The agent rammed into the Benz hard, causing it to slam into the bridge wall and erupt into flames on impact, engulfing King Jose in flames.

The other agents were shooting at the engine blocks of the Hummers as well as the tires, causing them to swerve recklessly and flip over the bridge wall into the Susquehanna River.

"Radio check, everyone still a go?" the lead agent questioned.

They all chimed back in: "All here, sir. Package still in tow."

The lead agent radioed in for chopper assistance and backup. But before he was able to finish, Turnpike Tito and his men showed up, boasting 9mm Uzis mounted on the sides of their motorcycles. All of his men fired on the trucks as they raced over the I-83 bridge. They rammed their trucks into the motorcycles while at the same time firing on each one and taking them out with head and body shots.

"Muthafucka, I got hit!" Tommy yelled out, feeling the hot metal burning his flesh.

Just as he was sitting up, the window shattered and exposed the passengers. Now they knew what truck he was in. The lead truck now had a dead agent who caught slugs to the face and neck, so this transit became hostile. All of the agents were feeling the urgency for backup. This was beyond any of their training and previous transits.

The agents narrowed down the shooters on the bikes to two, and the last two were still persistent, coming in fast and hard while shooting at the trucks.

"They're coming up on your left!" the agent in the back vehicle radioed to the agents with Tommy Guns in the truck.

Just as the bikes got close, the Suburban abruptly swerved hard and forced the bikes to crash into one another, causing them to both flip into the air high and slam down onto the concrete at a speed of one hundred-plus miles an hour. They were instantly killed as their bones broke and punctured their hearts and lung.

Turnpike Tito was driving fast with his silver .45mm automatic in hand with a pearl handle firing off at the truck that Tommy was in, trying to flatten the tires but not kill him. If anything, he would help Tommy escape, so he could get his money and/or product. Just as Tito was closing in, the agent switched lanes as the other agent's truck slowed down and forced Tito into a position, giving the agent a clear line of fire. Two center mass shots were fired into Tito's chest, killing him instantly and causing his body to become limp. His car went out of control as it crashed on the side of the highway.

Suddenly, the red Suburban exploded and flipped into the air as an RPG fired from a white cargo van with the Arab men in it. It was Amir's men chasing behind them, trying to finish what the others could not.

Agents in the remaining trucks returned fire upon seeing their fellow agents killed. At the same time, they were calling for backup. By now they didn't need to call. Many vehicles that witnessed this onslaught of gunfire had already called 911.

"Agent Davis, I'm in the sky. I see your convoy," the agent in the chopper said, now having eyes on their fellow agents. "Eyes open, the men in the van just took out another RPG. Don't let him get that shot off!" the agent said to his sniper in the chopper.

The sniper took aim at the Arab who was preparing to fire the RPG. He calmed his breathing finger on the trigger and waited for the helicopter to slow and steady, and then it happened. He squeezed the trigger, unleashing the 50-caliber slug that raced through the air and slammed violently into the Arab's skull, turning his brains, bones, and flesh into a pinkish mist as the life escaped him. However, it didn't take long before another Arab popped into the window and took hold of the RPG, firing it off and hitting the truck closest to it. It flipped into the air, only to erupt and crash back down to the ground with brute force, killing the agents inside. Tommy Guns and the agents in the remaining trucks feared the worst, knowing they too could be next.

Tommy also knew that it was them muthafuckas from the warehouse who were thinking that he and his cousins had seen something. But it was pure coincidence being in the wrong place at the wrong time.

The sniper fired off two back-to-back rounds, piercing the side of the van's passenger door and the head of the shooter, killing him instantly.

"That should be it with the RPG. I don't see anyone else attempting to grab at it," the sniper said, still taking aim while looking through his scope.

On the other hand, Amir was still being persistent wanting Tommy Guns dead. So, he mashed the gas of the Brabus 65AMG and made the V-12 engine accelerate the Benz as he demanded the remaining driver in the van to crash into the trucks. The driver did just that, only to be met with death as the melting barrage of bullets took hold of his flesh and sucked the life from his body.

Upon seeing this, Amir began firing off rounds from his weapon before pressing the pedal to the floor and taking the Brabus to an easy 150 MPH, gliding past the FBI agents on the ground but not the chopper.

After a few minutes into his high-speed flight, he realized he wasn't going anywhere with the roadblocks and chopper assisting in his capture. He brought his car to a slow halt before stopping.

"Allah u Akbar!" he said, after placing the gear in park.

He then checked the clip of his weapon and saw that he was being surrounded fast as cars blocked him in and agents jumped out of their cars to surround him with their guns drawn, ready to take him out if he made any sudden moves.

"Let me see your hands! Put your hands up!" agents yelled out.

He ignored them and looked ahead, thinking about his next move to get their attention.

The news choppers were now present filming the event as it unfolded, knowing it was about to get heated.

Mohamad was alerted by Rakman, who was now disappointed with the outcome of the situation. He asked his cousin to take care of it. He was looking on at the news as everyone else saw his cousin exiting the car with his weapon in hand.

"Put the gun down! Drop it, asshole, or you won't see tomorrow!" the adrenaline-pumped agent yelled with his finger pressing up against the trigger, ready to take this son of a bitch out.

To their surprise, Amir immediately placed the

gun to his own head. Rakman was at home coaching his cousin on as if he could hear him through the television.

"Do it in the name of Allah. I will see you in paradise. Allah u Akbar," Rakman said while staring deep into the TV and watching his cousin's every move.

Suddenly Amir yelled out, "Allah u Akbar! His will, will be done!"

He shifted his gun toward the agents, hoping to die by the gun. The agent he pointed at fired off two rounds. One slammed into the right shoulder of the hand in which he was holding the gun. The other slug hit him in the left thigh. The two slugs dropped him and the gun, giving the surrounding agents enough time to rush in kicking the .45mm away from him.

"That was real stupid to try something like that!" the agent said, flipping him over and cuffing him.

Rakman was pissed his cousin didn't kill himself. This only meant more problems. Tommy was still alive, and now his cousin was going to jail. As Rakman turned off the television, he knew that something had to be done.

Rakman's plans were now altered since his

cousin was a big part of the process. He needed to think fast. He would use Amir's capture as leverage.

The agents sought medical attention for Tommy Guns and Amir before hauling them off to jail. Tommy knew that it was over with Tito and Jose, or so he hoped. As for these Arab muthafuckas, they were relentless. Who knew what they would do next to take his life or anyone's around him.

CHAPTER 19

LATER THAT EVENING, TOMMY Guns found himself at York County Prison. It was a change of prisons since the convoy was attacked earlier. The FBI knew someone from the Dauphin County Prison was responsible for leaking the travel times and route to the Cumberland County Prison, so they made sure to send agents to the prison ASAP because this leak cost lives and jeopardized many more.

As agents sought questions over in Dauphin County, Federal agents hovered over Amir Hussein at the FBI Headquarters in Harrisburg. At the same time, Tommy Guns was being interrogated at York County by agents.

~ ~ ~

"Mr. Anderson, who the fuck were those guys that tried to break you out?" the agent asked, staring him me. I knew who the men were, but it wasn't my place to say a word. "You think your silence is going to save you from death row? We lost agents here!"

"You really think they were trying to break me out? I guess you didn't take notice of the bullet in my arm?" I said sarcastically.

"You may be right about Amir Hussein. His crew came hard as if they wanted you erased from this earth," Agent Johnson said.

His attention shifted upon seeing another agent pop his head into the room.

"Johnson."

"Yes, sir, Agent Smith," he responded while making his way over to the door.

The two agents whispered over by the door briefly before Agent Johnson made his way back over to me.

"It's crazy about the two guys in the fancy cars. We had their tags run. The Miami guy's a bigwig, from what our Florida agents tell us. His name was Tito Alverez, a.k.a. Turnpike Tito. They could never get close to him down there, but karma has its own plans. He came to us to meet his demise," Agent Johnson said, looking into my face while searching for telltale signs.

"As for the other guy, he was Jose Rodriguez aka King Jose from New York. You must have really pissed these two men off, or you're in debt to them? So now with their deaths, you inherit their riches?"

he added with a smirk.

This fucking agent was relentless in thinking he knew what the fuck was going on. I didn't give a fuck! I just gave a sadistic smirk. Besides, the money was in a safe place.

"You'll never get a chance to spend it! You'll fry on death row for the murder of Detective Corrnick. I'll make sure you get charged with the other agents' deaths too, you piece of shit!"

"Johnson! I know we lost men, but you're going off track, don't you think?" Agent Smith asked, bringing his co-worker back to the reason they were there. Before anyone could get in another word, an agent entered the room with a folder in his hand and more information about what was going on.

"Gentlemen, we have a bigger problem at hand. Amir Hussein is a member of Al-Qaeda. He's also in association with the Islamic Jihad Organization, IJO, a group of men who conduct terrorist operations around the world."

"This guy should have been on the CIA's watch list or ours, but he managed to stay under the radar," Agent Smith said.

"Our agents have him at headquarters interrogating him now, but he's trying to lawyer up and chanting 'Allah u Akbar,'" Agent Michaels said.

He was preparing to leave the room, when he added, "Figure out the connection between these men. Something is just not sitting right with this."

He then handed them the folder with pictures in it. The agents came back over to where I sat and placed the pictures on the table. The pictures were of Amir in the States as well as pictures of him in Saudi Arabia. They had all been taken by the CIA.

"I don't know this muthafucka other than seeing him today trying to take all of us out," I responded, lying through my teeth because I had seen him and his cousin two times before. It was their cars that stood out to me.

"From our profile on this guy, he is the total opposite of the other two that tried taking us out today. My mind is telling me that you know this guy somehow or some way," Agent Johnson said, not trusting me at all.

"Think what you want. I don't have anything to say," I responded, crossing my arms and becoming closed off to any other questions.

I knew the code of the streets. More importantly, what's done was done. Nothing that happened could be changed from this point.

CHAPTER 20

RAKMAN WAS SETTING PLAN C in motion after all of the chaos that went on, including his cousin now being in jail. He ordered the first of the cargo vans that were parked by the governor's mansion to be armed with explosives. They would await confirmation to detonate them. He also reached out to his soldiers in Middletown, PA, where the Three Mile Island nuclear plant is located. He placed them on standby as well. The final hour was nearing. He needed this to take place without any more errors or problems.

Rakman's goal was to get America's attention via the city of Harrisburg because the city of Washington, DC, would be off limits and hard to get to since the 9-11 incident. It would be next to impossible to secure any buildings in DC, so the next best location and targets were those he chose thus far, including TMI, because the structure alone would explode and spread far and wide, reaching DC anyway. Having these explosives in position gave him the strategic power he needed, and the most powerful asset is the element of surprise.

Rakman and his associates prepared to leave their current location to a more secure destination. He needed to be on the move anyway just in case the FBI started connecting the dots between him and his cousin. It would not take long once they ran his tags on his car, and then his name to known associates and family.

He was in an all-black cargo van with tinted windows to conceal him and his passengers.

"Allah will see us through this. Just stay focused," Rakman said to the men in the van. "Allah is the most merciful."

As Rakman continued giving his men pep, the FBI still were questioning Amir.

"What is the reason you were trying to kill all of my agents in that convoy?" the agent questioned. "What is your plan? Is there something else going on we need to know about?"

Amir was looking back at the agents in the room.

"You Americans don't understand anything. Your laws are for the white Americans only to live at ease. This is not justice, and this is why people terrorize this country and other countries like it. Your country always wants war. The president and men behind him are greedy men. They want power and control over oil that is not even in this country as if it is their right to impose on."

The agents were looking on at Amir sensing that something big was about to take place. It was his words and body language that indicated to the agents that he was feeling the upper hand when he was the one being interrogated.

"What do you mean by your statement?" the agent questioned, but to no avail.

"Allah will be the final judge of this. Allah u Akbar."

The agents were feeling like no resolve was coming their way, so they shifted their questioning.

"Mr. Hussein, why is it you tried to kill our inmate in transit?"

"Because he is nosey like the rest of you Americans."

Amir and Rakman did not realize that Tommy did not see anything. It was simply bad timing.

Amir suddenly snapped, "No one can stop us! No one will be able to prevent what is to come! Allah u Akbar!"

His tone of voice brought alarm to the agents in

the room. They knew something was going to happen, but what? The agents knew they had to take the next step in reaching out to their superiors.

~ ~ ~

At 11:30 p.m., the director of the FBI, Jack Ross, was at home asleep with his wife's warm body lying next to him, when his cell phone sounded off. The sound of a phone ringing at this hour was cause for alarm. He felt something was wrong as he turned to see the time on the clock. It was now 11:31 p.m. Jack was a forty-seven-year-old white male who stood six-foot-tall, with a medium build of two hundred pounds, and brown eyes. He lived in Maryland since it is close to Washington, DC.

"Jack Ross here."

"Sir, this is Agent Davis out of the Harrisburg, PA, office. We have a serious situation, sir," he said with urgency in his voice.

Upon hearing this, Jack sat up in his bed and then reached over to turn on the nightlight.

"What's the problem?" he asked, already dreading the answer.

"Sir, we have a man in custody by the name of Amir Hussein. He's a known IJO member with ties to Al-Qaeda. He was picked up today because of multiple attempts to kill someone we had in transit."

"Yes, I saw that on CNN. So, what's his story?"

"He indicated that there is something big that's going to happen soon, and we can't stop it. He spoke about DC and our president, which is what prompted this call."

"You did right. We don't need another 9-11!" Jack said as he stepped out of his bed knowing sleep would have to wait. "I take it we officially have a full-out terror plot on our hands?"

"Yes, sir. These men are heavily equipped, because in their attempt to take out our transit, they used RPGs. You can't just buy that over the counter."

"If this is the real deal, then a lot of people are about to get woken up. If anything, else takes place, I want to know about it," Agent Ross said, ending the call and knowing that vital calls now needed to be made.

At 11:40 p.m. Jack Ross did as he said he would and began making calls to people in DC. He was on the phone with the lead secret service agent and informed him of the call that he just had with his agent.

The call didn't last long because the other agencies needed to be informed. The Secret Service moved through the White House informing the president and first lady. It didn't take long before they decided to evacuate to a secured location.

Other high-ranking members in the government in DC were also informed of the high alert but were told to stay calm.

At midnight Jack Ross made a call to Governor Rendell of Pennsylvania, who was at home in the governor's mansion located on 2nd and Maclay Streets, in Harrisburg.

"Hello."

"Governor Rendell, this is director Jack Ross with the FBI."

"What gives me the pleasure to be awakened at this hour of the night?"

"Sir, we have a high-level terror threat that was made by a man who is in FBI custody in our Harrisburg office," Jack said, explaining to him the same details that were told to him.

After the call, the governor called for his head of secret service. He came to his room within seconds.

"How can I help you, sir?" the agent asked.

"The FBI director just called. We're on high terror alert. I need you and your men to do a sweep of the parameter. Anything that doesn't look right, I want to know about it."

"Yes, sir."

At 12:15 a.m. the governor's secret service did as he had requested them by taking out the men and dogs. The dogs were barking loud and echoing through the silent streets.

As they were walking up the side street approaching 2nd Street, the dogs continued barking loud as they closed in on the white cargo van, awaking the Arab man inside. He was one of Rakman's soldiers.

He opened his eyes and realized the sound of dogs meant someone else was also there, meaning secret service. They hadn't paid him any attention before because the van had fake government tags and decals. He was lying there with his 9mm in one hand and the detonator in the other hand. There was enough C-4 to level the mansion if he were closer, which he planned on doing when given the orders from Rakman.

"Allah u Akbar," he whispered, now feeling the

end coming with each barking sound coming from the dogs.

His heart was racing fast until he realized they were passing by as the sounds of dogs barking dissipated. He closed his eyes and drifted back off to sleep for now.

At 12:45 a.m. the FBI agents were preparing to take Amir to York County Prison to be held without bail and high-level supervision, and with no phone calls or visitors. He was now a risk to national security. So, there was no chance he would contact anyone else to make any moves that would terrorize the country. That mistake was made with other acts of terror, and they wouldn't make the same mistake.

By 1:00 a.m., after a long day and even longer time interrogating Tommy Guns, the agents were bringing the show to an end, until Agent Johnson came back into the room with pictures of Rakman Hussein. Seeing the pictures alerted Tommy. His eyes widened a little, which was enough to let them know he recognized him.

"I take it he looks familiar to you?"

"I don't know that muthafucka either. So y'all done here or what?"

"We know there is a connection between you and them. He's Amir's cousin. So, you know they're planning an act of terror, and you're telling us you don't know anything. But Amir Hussein just conveniently wanted you dead?"

"The wrong people get shot at all of the time. That's life in the city for you," Tommy responded.

What else could he say? The Feds pretty much had the answers they wanted, he figured. Besides, being a rat wasn't his style.

The FBI already ran all known associates of Amir, which is how they found Rakman and other associates. It was also how they located all of his businesses and warehouses.

The agents let Tommy go back to his cell at 1:15 a.m. while they prepared to raid Rakman's properties. This was serious and needed to be taken care of.

CHAPTER 21

AT 1:45 A.M. A slew of FBI agents stormed Rakman's house and warehouse on Industrial Road. His home in the Forest Hills Estates of Harrisburg was worth more than $1,000,000, boasting over seven thousand square feet. Although it was a large house to look through, these agents were looking forward to it. They started going through all of his computers looking for a trail of evidence that might give some hint as to what they were planning to terrorize. One of the agents came across a map with locations circled; the first was in Middletown while the other locations were bunched together across Harrisburg. The agent immediately got the attention of the others, who were all frantically searching.

"Hey, guys, what do you think these circled locations represent?" Agent Smith asked.

"The three locations in the city could be the capitol, or it also could be the mansion. That's the only government establishments that crossed my mind," Agent Charles said, offering up his opinion.

"You might be right. The third circle here in

Middletown could be Three Mile Island. If so, this is not good for the surrounding cities," Agent Smith said while reaching for his cell phone to call TMI and Harrisburg International Airport (HIA).

He made them aware of what he had discovered so they would be on alert. He also told them to keep a low profile with this info, so they wouldn't scare anyone off.

As they continued to look through the house, they discovered a phone number that had Dauphin County Prison written at the top of it. His heart started beating faster, realizing what had taken place with the convoy. Seeing the name on the paper also confirmed to them that there was an inside man, captain Faris Mohamad. The agent quickly made the others aware of this newfound information.

While the agents at Rakman's house continued to search, other agents did the same over at his warehouse on Industrial Road. It didn't take long before they discovered bomb paraphernalia, wiring, casings, dynamite, nails, and pipes they chose not to use. Upon finding this, Agent Johnson signaled the others to make them aware of it.

"This is obviously where everything was put

ALL EYES ON TOMMY GUNZ

together. Now we need to find out where they took it from here. Fan out and see what else we can find that'll point in the direction they may be going."

"Hey, guys, over here!" the rookie agent yelled out.

They all rushed over to where the agent's voice came from. As they closed in, it was obvious what he was calling out for. There lay a body saturated in blood due to the bullets that riddled his body. Agent Johnson recognized his face. It was captain Faris Mohamad from the prison.

"Continue searching while I call Agent Smith."

"Agent Smith here."

"Smith, this is Johnson. I have your boy Faris Mohamad here."

"Good, hold him until I get there."

"I don't think he's in any hurry to meet you. Someone filled him up with bullets."

"So, they killed him to cover their tracks because there is evidence here linking him to the prison, which clearly was our leak," Agent Smith said. "If anything, else comes up, let me know."

As the call ended, another agent's voiced boomed through the air.

"Sir, over here! I think I got something worth looking at."

The agents all moved in with their guns drawn, just in case something else came at them as they approach to see what the agent discovered. Once they came into the aisle where he stood, they lowered their weapons. They found fake license plates, decals to government jobs, and more.

"These men are going to easily pass as government officials without question. Not good," Agent Johnson said, after realizing these explosives would be smuggled into areas full of politicians.

He called Agent Smith and made him aware of what he had found out. They both knew that director Jack Ross would have to be informed of this.

Jack Ross was in the midst of falling asleep again at 2:45 a.m. when his phone sounded off. He came out of the little sleep he was trying to get. At the same time, his heart was racing, knowing a call at this hour meant something else was wrong.

"Jack Ross speaking."

"Sir, this is Agent Smith from the Harrisburg office again. Sorry to wake you, but we came across more intel about this terror plot."

Hearing this only meant Jack needed to get out of

bed, because sleep was not going to happen now.

"Tell me what you discovered," Jack said.

"Washington is a distraction from what they're planning, sir. From the map we found at Rakman's home along with the bomb leftovers we came across, it all points to this city."

"So the places circled on the map, have you found those locations? More important, have these places been informed?"

"We're handling this as we speak. The targets, to my knowledge, are TMI or HIA. There are others in the city, but we figure with the fake uniforms and government tags they'll target our capitol here and/or the governor's mansion."

Hearing this was even more shocking and disturbing than Jack expected.

"Three Mile Island is already secured unless they find a way in, and we cannot allow that to happen," he paused while getting out of the bed and grabbing his pants. "Jesus, TMI! That would be a nuclear disaster. Thank you and your men for doing a good job. Now we have to stop this terrorist attack before it happens. Call me with any other leads or updates," Jack said before hanging up the phone.

His nerves were getting the best of him as he

feared the worst.

By 3:00 a.m. Agent Johnson and his men approached an office inside the warehouse to see if they could find out anything more about Rakman and his men. As the agent closed in on the door, a sudden blast of gunfire erupted. The noise alerted all agents at the same time the slugs came through the door and crashed into the agent's chest, forcing him off his feet and thrusting him backward.

The other agents instantly returned fire into the office where two Arab men found themselves barricaded.

The Arab men killed Mohamad as ordered, and then they awaited further instructions. In the process they fell asleep until the voices of the agents woke them up. Now they were cornered with AK-47s, ready to die but also kill as many Americans as they could.

The Arab goon tossed a grenade through the office window which landed by multiple agents.

"Grenade!" the agents yelled.

Suddenly the explosion became deafening as the blast spread fast, with shrapnel immediately killing three agents and wounding the others in close proximity. The blast turned up the heightened awareness of the agents as their adrenaline streamed through their bodies.

The gunfire continued until the agents stopped to reload. At the same time, the Arab men flipped their clips around to have a fully stocked fifty magazine in their AK-47s.

"Come out with your hands up!" Agent Johnson yelled. "No one else has to die. You come out now, and you don't have to end up like your friend."

"You Americans are stupid! We will all be dead before the night ends, just like that piece of shit you found in the warehouse!"

"It doesn't have to be this way!"

They didn't respond; however, the agents could hear the AK-47s being loaded and slugs being chambered. Agent Johnson signaled his men to close in but keep a tight parameter. As the men closed in, a voice came out of the room.

"I am coming out, don't shoot!"

No one responded because all of the agents knew something was wrong with the sudden change of heart. This only made them even more alert.

The door cracked open as the Arab man was peeking out. "Don't shoot; I come out."

There was no response from the agents as they

were too focused on the Arabs' next move.

The door opened all the way as he stood there with his hands behind his head along with a sadistic smirk on his face. The agents still didn't trust him, and they wouldn't until he was in handcuffs. He took a few steps out of the room and made his way toward the agents in front of him. At that moment, the other agents on the right and left side of the door, roughly ten to fifteen feet away, noticed his hands were not interlocked behind his head. He was holding a grenade.

"Grenade!" the agents all yelled in unison.

At the same time the Arab was about to toss the grenade at the agents, the other Arab came charging out of the room spraying the AK-47. However, he was met with a barrage of bullets that sucked the life from him and his friend. Their bodies fell to the floor with no more hope of terrorizing anyone else in this world. The agents rushed in over the two Arab men and pumped them with more gunfire. Their faces were disfigured from the slugs that took chunks of their flesh and bones away.

"Pieces of shit! They deserve the death that came to them!" one of the agents said while spitting on their bodies.

CHAPTER 22

IT WAS 4:00 A.M., and Jack Ross just finished up with all the calls he needed to make to the government officials in Washington, DC. They also needed to be informed of what was going on so they, too, could be secure in the buildings they were in.

After the calls, he started preparing to meet up with the agents in Harrisburg, when his wife woke from all of the movement in the house.

"Honey, how long do you think you'll be gone for?" she asked, knowing his job took him out of town quite often.

"I really don't know this time; however, I will stay in touch because of the girls' birthday," he said, knowing his twin daughters would be upset if he couldn't make it to their sweet sixteen.

"Be safe and know the girls and I love you."

"That's enough love to come back home to, babe," he responded, leaning in to give her a kiss before leaving the room.

He knew that this national security matter was urgent and needed his attention now, so he would use the FBI's jet to get to Harrisburg. This would give him the much-needed time to think and focus, so he could approach the situation strategically.

~ ~ ~

At 5:00 a.m. Rakman was preparing to make salat with his followers before they continued on with the events of the day that would get America's attention. The mood was beyond serious. These men were mentally, emotionally, and physically committed to the end game they had planned.

Rakman knew he couldn't stay here long because of the surrounding events that had taken place thus far. The FBI would also target this location once they figured he was the owner.

At 6:00 a.m. Rakman decided to make a call to the FBI Headquarters in Harrisburg using a secured phone that would scramble any attempt to trace his location. This equipment came from one of his good associates that worked in higher-level government. The phone's signal would lead them astray by bouncing off multiple cell towers.

"Agent Anderson speaking, how may I help you?"

"This is Rakman Hussein. By now you may have

ravished every one of the properties I have, but that is not why I am calling," he began as Agent Anderson waved to the others in the room to get their attention to the call. "If my cousin is not released in the hour and placed on a plane by himself out of this country, I will set my first example."

Agent Anderson tried to negotiate, but the call ended abruptly. Rakman knew he only had two minutes tops per call.

The FBI was now at odds at having to figure out what their next move would be, since America was not one for negotiating with anyone, let alone terrorists.

Back at his location, Rakman was now ready to leave and move his plan forward.

"Allah will lead you to paradise as long as you do not stray from His plans," Rakman said to his soldier leaving him to go as discussed.

"As-salamu alaykum, brother."

"Walaikum assalam, and may Allah be with you in your final moment," Rakman said while exiting with the other soldier.

They left in the all-black cargo van with new decals on it as they headed to their destination.

~ ~ ~

At 6:45 a.m. Governor Rendell and his wife were preparing to leave the mansion to a more secure and unknown location. But first the secret service was doing a parameter check to make sure no one was waiting to take them out.

With the newfound information of fake decals being used, the secret service called in on a van they took notice of earlier that night. After running the tags and checking the log for maintenance, nothing was on file for these fraudulent tags and decals. Right then they all became alert and closed in on the van. The first of the four secret service agents closed in on the driver's side door, after noticing that the keys were still in the ignition, but the door was locked.

He signaled to the others to let them know the situation. Another secret service member came up on the van's back doors and looked through the window, where he immediately noticed that someone was inside asleep.

"Sir, are you okay in there?" he asked while knocking on the window to wake the Arab man who was in a deep sleep.

As the Arab man opened his eyes, he immediately felt that he was busted by the dogs sniffing him out since they were barking earlier. Suddenly he took hold of his 9mm and fired off shots, catching the secret service agents off guard. They instantly took cover before returning a burst of fire. In between shots being fired, they could hear the man inside the truck speaking Arabic and shouting out in between firing at the agents.

"Come out with your hands up! There is no way out of this situation!" the agents yelled out.

"Allah is the way out of this situation!" he sounded off, reloading his weapon to continue firing back at the agents.

"Go around to the front to see if you can get a better shot at this guy," the secret service agent told his partner.

He did just that, and he ran around to the front of the van looking through the front of the window and seeing his target. He took aim and fired off two back-to-back shots that raced through the air into the van, pounding into the flesh of the Arab man and piercing his lung. The hit caused him to drop his gun as he was reaching for his chest. His eyes widened in panic from the sudden blow from the bullets sucking the air from his lungs. This was the end, he thought, so he grabbed the detonator that armed the C-4 explosives and then placed his thumb on the button as he made his final prayer to Allah.

The agents closed in, shattering the windows on the van while unlocking the front doors. The Arab man could hear them closing in, so he closed his eyes and forced these words from his mouth, "Allah knows best."

At that very moment, he pressed the button which unleashed death on all of those agents present. The blast roared and erupted, engulfing everything in its path. The sound wave shattered the windows of the houses around it and shook all the vehicles within a block's range and caused their alarms to go off. The explosion also left a hole in the ground where the van continued to burn. Fire hydrants erupted and sprayed water with force into the air. The sound of the explosion could be heard for a mile in radius.

On the other side of the mansion, the governor and his family were being driven away in a bullet-proof limo to a secured location. As the limo drove down Front Street, the governor looked back and could see smoke in the air. At the same time, he could hear the fire trucks blaring their sirens as they rushed toward the scene.

This act of terror wouldn't go unpunished.

CHAPTER 23

RAKMAN PLACED ANOTHER CALL to the FBI at 7:00 a.m. He wanted to know if there was an update on his cousin's release.

"Agent Anderson speaking, how can I help you?"

"Has the FBI released my cousin yet?"

Agent Anderson was thinking about the explosion he was made aware of at the governor's mansion. So, he knew the threat was real.

Agent Anderson was trying to speak with confidence knowing he hadn't tried one bit to get his cousin out of jail.

"We're working on it as we speak," he replied.

"You fucking Americans just don't get it, do you? You will never understand until it is too late, and the end is near, and everyone is in the fire begging to be saved!" Rakman was furious. "I gave you more than enough time. If he is not released, this city will burn!" he yelled before he hung up and left Agent Anderson to process his capability of destruction fully.

~ ~ ~

At 7:15 a.m. the town of Middletown, PA, was now on high alert. The national guard also came in to assist at the TMI area as well as the airport in order to make certain that no one would get a chance to destroy those structures.

The Arab soldiers Rakman sent to fulfill their destiny were now aware of all the security around the area, especially after the national guard arrived. The Arab man called Rakman to make him aware of the situation.

"My brother, the time has come sooner than you may have wanted it. These Americans have their national guard here."

"Allah is the most merciful, and He knows it is time. I'll see you in paradise. As-salamu alaykum!" Rakman said, knowing he would never speak to them again.

"Walaikum assalam," he said, upon hanging up the phone before arming the explosives. He was ready to meet his maker.

Rakman was loading up his twin nickel-plated .45mms with the pearl handles and the inscription *Allah u Akbar*.

He was thinking about his next step if the FBI did

not release his cousin.

The men at the capitol were also at the ready with explosives armed and detonator in hand.

~ ~ ~

Back in Middletown, the Arab goons were just finishing up their final prayer. Then one of them started up the van, revving up the gas and pressing down on the pedal to race toward the nuclear plant. The front gate was being secured by military Hummers. This didn't stop him, since his foot was all the way down on the floor. It was the final moment closing in fast as he clenched the detonator in his hand with his thumb on the button. The national guard members saw the van approaching fast. They took aim at the van and then realized it wasn't going to slow down, so they unleashed a barrage of bullets.

"Allah! Allah u Akbar!" the men yelled out.

They were within a few feet before impact and detonation. Suddenly, as the drive pressed the button, time seemed to slow as they came crashing into the military vehicles, followed by a brute explosion, the blinding light of fire, shrapnel, and a violent blast that tore through the air. All in its path sucked the life from anyone or anything within a fifty-yard radius. The vehicles surrounding the immediate blast became scrap as they were forced apart. The reinforced gates still stood with a slight bend in the metal. The blast sent a wave of unforgiving destruction as the ground and all around it shook. It could be heard for miles.

The remaining national guard member that wasn't in the immediate blast area survived. They assisted one another in between calling for more backup and medical attention. As for any attempt on TMI, the silos are four to six feet of thick concrete and steel, so it would have been a feat for them to get through that, even if they did make it past security.

It didn't take long before news crews came to tell their version of events from what they had seen and gathered from survivors.

CHAPTER 24

RAKMAN WAS ON THE phone calling the FBI once again. Only this time he had even more leverage since his soldiers took their stand in Middletown by setting off the explosives.

"Agent Smith here," he answered.

"Mr. Smith, do I have you Americans' attention, or need I impose more destruction on this city and country? Your partner Agent Anderson realized he's not in the position to or even capable of filling my demands."

"That's neither here or there, but you now have my attention as well as the director of the bureau Jack Ross's. He's here to help us all get some understanding and resolve this situation," Agent Smith responded.

As the call went on, the FBI's counterintelligence unit was trying to trace the scrambled call, so they could zero in on Rakman's location. The problem is he did not stay on the phone long enough for the trace to be complete.

After Rakman again demanded the release of his

cousin, he hung up the phone. He was gone without a trace.

Jack Ross stood up and took control over the operation.

"Listen up, ladies and gentlemen. We have lost too many men and women because of this terrorist scum. I want him captured. We need him to believe that we're going to release his cousin. The moment we locate his cell phone, we'll bring him down; and both of these terrorists will be prosecuted. This is not a game. We have lives at stake, so think ahead to catch this guy." Jack paused, scanning the faces of his agents and allowing his words to sink in. "I need a team to get his cousin from York County Prison ASAP and get him on the phone as soon as he in transit. We want to sell this to his cousin until he's in cuffs."

The agents all went to do their jobs as assigned to them. Rakman was on the other side of the city, where he sat and thought about his next target.

As he was collecting his thoughts, he could hear the roaring of F-16 fighter jets flying overhead. They were ready to take out any threats in the sky that came close to the state capitol or TMI, as well as in the nation's capitol.

~ ~ ~

At exactly 10:00 a.m. the guard yelled, "York County Prison inmate Tom Anderson!" which woke me up.

I jumped up fast as shit. I was still shell-shocked and alert from all the bullshit that had been going on in my life.

"What the fuck y'all want?" I said.

"You're getting transferred in an hour, so get your shit together."

"Why are y'all moving me. This shit is stupid."

"You're a high-profile inmate, plus a lot of people want you dead from the looks of things," the CO said, really adding his own version of why, since he really didn't know shit.

"So, my visit is not going to happen today? These some stupid muthafuckas!" I snapped, knowing it would take thirty minutes for my mom to get down here.

"I'll give you a two-minute call to cancel it," the CO responded.

They gave me the call; however, in the process, I reached out to some cats I came across, to check their loyalty and gangster. After the call, I made my way back to the cell to get all my shit together before lying back and thinking about the last few weeks and the life I was living with my cousins, the Miami connect, and the New York connect. Life was good. Now I was on my own without my cousins, who were like my thugged-out homies and paper chasers.

~ ~ ~

At 10:30 a.m. Rakman was making sure his team in the black cargo made it to their location.

"Aki, are you in position?"

"Yes, brother, I'm here waiting on the final moment and your call."

"Is the other aki in place?"

"He's also in place, and ready to be greeted by Allah."

"Good, I'll call you when it is time; however, if you don't hear from me, then go on without me, and I'll see you in paradise. As-salamu alaykum."

"May peace be unto you, my brother," he responded before hanging up the phone.

Becoming impatient, Rakman called up the Feds again. The phone rang a few times before the line was picked up.

"Agent Smith here."

"I could let the phone ring one hundred times and you stupid Americans wouldn't be able to trace it, so stop wasting time that you could be getting my cousin out! Where is he?"

Agents were scrambling to get Amir on the phone to speak with his cousin.

"We're going to have your cousin call you as soon as he exits the prison."

"I'll believe it when it's done. You Americans will regret this day if you do not comply with this simple request," Rakman said after he hung up and left the agents to think about the reality of what was going on and the lives that would end if they failed to meet his demands.

As he hung up, the agents picked up Amir and placed Agent Smith in contact with him.

"Amir, Agent Smith speaking. We're trying to arrange that you speak with your cousin as soon as he calls back."

"If you people try anything, I will let him know."

"No one is going to try anything. We just want to bring an end to all of these people killing themselves and others in the process," Agent Smith said, referring to the suicide bombers.

Agent Smith was on the phone at 10:45 a.m. as another agent signaled to make him aware that Rakman was calling again.

"Patch the call through to this line," he said. Then he added, "Amir, we're connecting you and your cousin now."

"Rakman, we have your cousin on the line," he said before he then allowed the men to speak.

"As-salamu alaykum, Amir."

"Allah is great, and you, my cousin, not leaving me behind is a blessing in itself," Amir said, feeling good about this possibility of freedom.

"Where are you now, Amir?"

"I'm on I-83 coming toward Harrisburg."

"Okay! Agent Smith, have your men pull over once they get in the middle of the bridge. I know you have agents following this vehicle, so I want the agents in the truck with Amir to exit and leave my cousin alone. If anyone approaches or follows Amir, then I will have my men set off another explosion to a valuable asset to your country," Rakman threatened before he hung up, knowing his time was running out to evade the trace.

The agents did as requested after the call. On the other hand, Jack Ross was pissed with the sudden plans.

"I didn't see that coming. Get a chopper in the sky and tell the agents tailing to keep their distance."

Rakman reached out to his men at the capitol building and redirected them to now go pick up Amir. They did just that, checking all of their fully automatic weapons. They were ready to protect Amir by any means. They did not want to let Rakman down. At the same time, they believed that all of this was in the name of Allah.

"It's time for me to meet up with Amir," Rakman said to his associate with him.

CHAPTER 25

AT 11:00 A.M. TWO all-black Yukon Denalis with dark tinted windows carrying two agents in each truck came to me up. "Inmate Tom Anderson. It's time for your transfer." This was a more secure and tight transfer. In fact, they were in and out, driving fast and alert.

Instinct is a muthafucka, America. There was something not right about the agents that came to get me. They didn't even put a vest on me like they had previously done. Also, there were two trucks this time, when four were not enough the first time. Plus, the agent in the passenger seat kept looking back at me like I was the one with the gun.

The inside of the truck didn't look anything like the other truck, and something was really up with these agents. Is this the CIA or somebody who thinks I really know something?

"Yo, where the fuck are y'all taking me?"

There was nothing but silence as they turned to each other and then ignored the shit out of me. My heart was beating a little faster now, because my hood instinct was telling me that shit was about to go south from here.

"Oh, you deaf or you need each other's permission to speak? Is that your bitch or something?" I said, obviously pissing them off.

At the same time I leaned forward and saw that their IDs were bogus as a muthafucka. I looked down and braced myself mentally for what I was about to do, because I wasn't about to let these fake-ass cop niggas get at me.

Suddenly it came to me. My cuffs. I raised my hands up over the passenger seat and wrapped the cuffs around this fake-ass nigga's neck and choked him. He instantly started kicking around, feeling the air drain from his lungs.

"Shoot him! Shoot this asshole!" he managed to get out as I adjusted my grip.

"You muthafuckas is going to die for this shit!" I said while squeezing harder.

His face was showing it all, but he couldn't do anything about it. He took his gun from the holster and tried to shoot me, but he feared the death that was coming his way fast. He started shooting recklessly. A few slugs raced through the air and slammed into the head of the driver in the front truck, killing him instantly and causing the truck to swerve violently before crashing. I squeezed harder. I wanted this nigga to die now because his wide shooting was causing slugs to fly past my head, and I was not feeling this shit. He shook violently once more as my grip tightened and the life escaped him, just as he let out a lifeless grunt. Right then his partner was reaching for his gun, so I ducked behind the driver's seat making it hard for this nigga to take me out.

I was thinking about choking out this muthafucka, too, but that would mean crashing, and that wasn't a good look. As those thoughts came to me, slugs pierced the driver's door and hit him in the ribs.

"Son of a bitch!" the fake agent let out.

I looked out the window and saw that it was the little Spanish nigga I had contacted during my brief call, driving alongside the truck. His all-white Land Rover sat on 24s and had a faded mirror tint.

"Pull over, punta, ahora!" the Spanish nigga told him.

He did just that, knowing the end for him would be death if he did not. I had told the little Spanish homie I would give him one hundred stacks if he could cause a diversion or something.

With all of the fully automatic weapons pointed at this cat driving the van, he pulled over quickly. The little homie and his team jumped out and quick-rushed over to the truck, opening the back door. The other van driver, seeing that he didn't have a chance against this crew, didn't stop, but drove by sending a few bullets out the passenger window at us, without any collateral damage.

"Yo, Tommy Guns, you good, *hermano*?"

"Yeah, hurry up and get the key from this dead muthafucka right here."

He got the key and quickly took off the cuffs. His team had guns pointing at this fake-ass cop.

Rico was the Spanish nigga I'm talking about. He was in the county with me before he made bail. The homie stood five foot eleven. He had slicked-back hair and brown eyes, and he was closely shaven and even had his eyebrows tweezed. That's some Puerto Rican shit, but this nigga and his crew are real, and I fuck with that.

"Who put you and the rest of these fake-ass agents up to this?" I asked the fake cop.

I needed an answer quickly because we had to get the fuck out of there.

"Rakman Hussein promised us a quarter of a million each to bring you to him alive. I guess you're that important to him?"

"That's what his dumb ass thinks. Where the fuck is he?" I asked, wanting to kill him for the many attempts on my life.

"I don't know where he is. He said he'd call this phone within the hour," he responded while taking the phone from his pocket.

I snatched the phone from him and then looked back at him with murderous eyes.

"Was it worth it, you stupid muthafucka?"

Before he could respond, Rico blasted him with a headshot.

"Hermano, we don't have time for this shit. Let's go," Rico said, running back to his truck.

We all jumped in ready to go. As we accelerated toward Harrisburg, Rico introduced me to his team.

"Hermano, this is my blood in/blood out crew. From right to left, my homeboy is Chino, who I've known since we were kids. Flaco is my little brother, and Angel is my brother's best friend. We keep a tight circle, you know."

"Oye, that punta was scared once he seen us," Angel said, all hyped up.

He really reminded me of a Spanish version of my cousin, Ace.

"Rico, I got y'all on the bread, too. I keep my word, you feel me?"

"I know, hermano. You connected for real, bro. Plus you about that money."

"We going to spend that one hundred stacks on vacation, bro?" Angel said, thinking about all of the women he was going to be with while balling out of control.

"Puerto Rico is where we going with all of those crazy sexy-ass Latinas, bro," Chino said with a smile.

Rico was merging onto the I-83 highway heading toward Harrisburg to take me to get my money, so I could look out for these niggas. I can't lie. They really held me down, and if I could put a team together to take over a city, it would be with these cats.

As we were crossing the I-83 bridge, I noticed a truck off to the side with someone sitting in the driver's seat. Where the truck was located was not normal, so it stood out since it was parked in the middle of the bridge. Oh shit, it's that Arab muthafucka, Amir, I was thinking as we were passing by.

"What the fuck is he doing?" I said aloud.

"Who is that, hermano? He a problem or what?" Angel asked, with his gun at the ready.

"That's Amir Hussein, the muthafucka that tried to kill me when the fellas came to get me from Dauphin County."

"How is he out already? We can pull over, and back up all the way and kill him."

"Fuck that piece of shit. We don't have time for him. We got to get this money, and I got to get the fuck out of this city," I said.

But it was crazy seeing this piece of shit. That's why I knew they had different money.

"Rico, get off up there at the 13th Street exit," I said.

It was time to go to my stash house to pay these niggas for their thugged-out services.

It didn't take long before we made it to my spot. I jumped out of the whip and knocked on the door. Shari better answer this door, I thought as I waited. I had Turnpike Tito's $600,000, King Jose's 750 stacks, and product left. There were fifty kilos to be exact.

She opened the door shocked to see me, since I wasn't supposed to be out.

"Tommy, what are you doing here?" she asked in disbelief.

I walked right past her and down to the basement.

"I can't really explain right now, but I got to hurry up." I moved the dryer to expose the safe in the wall. I had that shit custom built. Although that shit looked like a brick wall, it was my safe. I grabbed six vacuum-sealed bags containing $100,000 each. Then I put everything back as it was before taking a pillowcase to put the money in. I went back upstairs with Shari. She came up to me and began kissing and hugging on me.

"I love you, Tommy."

"I know, but I can't stay right now. Shit's crazy, but I'll call you in a few days," I said, kissing her soft lips.

"Be safe and know me and your sons love you."

"I'll send for you. Just be patient and let me get grounded," I said. She knows how I live.

I ran back out to the truck and jumped in, pulling out four of the vacuum-sealed bags. They all became excited since they had never seen this amount of money before.

"This is for you and your team. I got love and respect for all of y'all," I said. "Take me to the bus station, so I can get out of this city," I added.

"Damn, we hood rich, hermanos," Angel said, tearing open the bag of money and fanning the $100 bills. "We going to get plenty of señoritas with this cash," he added.

It was exactly noon when the fake agent's cell phone rang. I knew it was Rakman, so I had Rico and his team quiet down for a second.

"Hold up, y'all. It's this muthafucka that tried to take me out," I said before pressing the Accept button. "Hello, you stupid muthafucka." He was shocked to hear my voice and tone. "Your fake-ass Fed friends are dead just like you would be if I had the time," I said.

"You idiot! You caused me a lot of money and disrupted what we have going on."

"Fuck you and your money. If I had more time, I would track you down and blow your fucking brains out. But God and bad timing are on your side right now," I said, hanging up the phone and not allowing him to get in another word. Besides, it's time to get out of this city before it's too late.

I got Rico's info, so I could reach out to him when I got situated. Then he dropped me off, so I could leave the city. I didn't know where to, but I needed to go somewhere and stay low for a long while.

CHAPTER 26

AT 12:30 P.M. RAKMAN'S Arab goons arrived on the I-83 bridge to secure Amir. Amir saw his Muslim brothers jump out of the truck and rush over to the van. Another van followed behind for back up.

"As-salamu alaykum, Amir."

"May peace unto you, my brothers. Is everything going as planned?" he asked.

"It's going even better now that you're in the picture. Allah is great."

"Good, very good. We will have all that we please and see one another in the end in paradise."

The cell phone chimed in, getting their attention. It was Rakman calling his soldier's phone to check on the status of his cousin. The Arab man passed the phone to Amir.

"It's Rakman."

"Allah knows best, and I am grateful for you and him," Amir said to his cousin.

"I did what you would have done for me."

"What is our next move?" Amir asked, getting back to business, knowing that time was not on their side with the FBI probably tailing him.

"All of our men are in place. I tried to have that black drug dealer brought to us, but to no avail. He has luck on his side."

"His time will come. Right now, we can't lose focus. I'll have these men set back up at the capitol or another location to make sure all is done," he said upon ending the call.

The van following Amir for backup radioed to make him aware that they were being followed by way of chopper. Amir looked up and saw the helicopter. Even though it was so high, they blew their cover. At the same time, he called his cousin back to let him know he was being followed.

"What's going on?" Rakman asked, knowing a return call this fast was not good news.

"These stupid Americans have a helicopter following us. I'll have these men take me to the airport. I have something planned," he said, looking around to see if any vehicles were also being discrete and trying to follow. They were, but he did not notice them just yet.

"Should we arm the explosives?" the Arab soldier asked.

"Yes, we must stay ready to carry out this mission. Allah will lead the way."

As Amir and his men prepared for the end, back at the FBI headquarters, Jack Ross was stressing to his agents in the chopper not to lose sight of the van.

"Keep that van close. We need to take him and his cousin down to bring this shit to an end," he said before he turned to Agent Smith. "Smith, get your men ready to take down these scums."

"Yes, sir, we got this!" Agent Smith said as he and Agent Anderson gathered men to leave.

There was now a total of sixteen agents in four Suburban trucks. Agent Johnson stayed back to help Director Ross track down Rakman's cell phone signal. Jack Ross had his best guys working on the this.

"Sir, I got it," one of the specialists yelled out, referring to Rakman's cell signal.

Jack and Agent Johnson rushed over and wanted to know where he was located.

"What do you have?" Jack asked.

"I triangulated his position pinging off the cell towers here and here."

"Hold up! So, what does this tell me? I want to

know his exact location," Jack said with urgency, knowing they were up against time.

"I got it, sir. I was getting to that," he responded as Agent Johnson gathered his men to leave.

Amir was approaching the airport when his cousin called.

"We have a change of plans," Amir said.

"What do you mean?"

"The Americans are playing their games and following us in the helicopter. Now I'm going to the airport with a new destination for the end."

Rakman really could feel the end coming near for him and his cousin.

"Allah will guide us to the end. I'll see you in paradise, Amir."

"Allah u Akbar."

The call ended as the seriousness of the end set in as the vans came onto the HIA property.

"Go to the main terminals," Amir directed his men.

There, the men discussed what their intent was going to be as well as everyone's target. Amir was now strategically thinking. As the van stopped, they were all in conversation ready to move out, until an airport officer knocked on the window. At the same time, the agents in the helicopter saw them parked by the main entrance. They realized that the van might also be equipped with explosives. They radioed Agent Smith to make him aware of their location, since he and his team were only minutes away.

Seeing the officer at his window spiked Amir's heart, making it race fast. Is this it? Should I kill him and everyone around? he thought, before rolling down the windows.

"What's the problem, officer?"

"You can't park here. This area is for drop-offs only."

"We got sidetracked. We'll move now," he responded.

The officer made his way back to the other van to tell him the same thing. When he tapped on the van's window, his eyes roamed to the back of the van where he saw some movement. An Arab man was loading a fully automatic assault rifle.

Immediately, the officer's mind and heart raced as he took a step back and reached for his sidearm, taking it from the holster. In that same moment, the Arab man in the passenger seat took his Glock

.40mm and fired off two rounds that spit fire and hot melting slugs into the officer's face, twisting his head as the brains ejected through his skull. As his body was falling, everyone in the area became alerted by the roaring of the gun, which caused them to run frantically and take cover. In the same instance, the other Arab men exited the van with guns in hand at the ready, especially after seeing multiple airport police approaching fast with their guns out. Bullets slammed into the cars around them as well as the officers.

Amir saw that officers were wearing bullet-proof vests, because he shot a few of them center mass, only for them to pop back up and shoot back at him.

"Take all head shots. They're wearing vests!"

Agent Smith and his team closed in on the airport fast after hearing about the gunfight. They were practically in the middle of the situation as they came upon the property.

Amir saw the Feds arrive, so he yelled, "Keep them at bay!"

Amir jumped back into the van and took hold of the detonator in one hand and the steering wheel in the other. He then mashed the gas and raced to war to the airstrip where planes were loading passengers.

The FBI knew there were enough explosives to take out a few planes if detonated, especially if they had the same amount as the previous explosion site.

Agent Smith drove fast and ran over one of the Arab men in the process of going through the barrage of bullets. His focus was on Amir in the van. He could not let him get away or detonate the explosives. The other Arab men continued fighting with the airport police and other agents. A grenade was tossed by one of the Arab goons that slid under one of the agent's truck, causing the truck to lift up and slam down hard from the explosion. At the same time, an agent ended up dead, with a few injured from the shrapnel.

After the eruption from the grenade settled, the remaining agents returned fire and took out three of the Arab men with military precision, center mass, piercing their hearts and dropping them in the midst of their actions. The last of the Arab men ran toward the cargo van, where the detonator for the C-4 was inside. He figured if he could get to it, he could set it off. But those thoughts came to a halt as slugs chased him down, crashing into his legs and back while thrusting up against the van before he slid down to the ground land lay wounded on his stomach.

The agents closed in fast when they saw the man struggling to breathe and speak at the same time. They turned him over, only to discover a grenade in his hand with the pin already out of it. As they yelled out a warning, they also tried to retreat, but it was too late. The grenade exploded, blowing the agents back with hot shards of metal and tearing away at their flesh. The explosion took their lives before their bodies even hit the ground. The Arab man's body was in pieces because he took the brunt of the blast. His arm was on the roof of the van while the other parts of his body spread out.

Agent Smith was hurt but knew he did not have time to stop. He needed to get Amir before any more lives were taken. The chopper kept Agent Smith updated on Amir's location and allowed him to close in on the van he was in. Amir was parked in between two 747 Boeing passenger planes with hundreds of civilians on them.

He held the detonator in his hand knowing the end was near.

The FBI closed in on the van and surrounded him

while the chopper's sniper was already looking through his scope with a clean line of sight. He was ready on the orders to take out the suspect.

"Agent Smith, I have eyes on the target. He has the detonator in his hand," the sniper said.

"Keep him locked in and take him out if he looks to be making any sudden moves. I'm going to try to talk him out of this," he said as he got out of the truck with hands up and no gun, just his vest on.

"Amir Hussein, let's talk about what it is you and your cousin want!" he yelled out, taking steps closer and closer.

His heart started beating fast up against his chest as he realized what he was getting himself into. This crazy son of a bitch could easily detonate the bomb, taking him out as well as the passengers on the planes. This would be bad, but Agent Smith was willing to take a chance and talk him down to get some resolve.

Agent Smith's forehead was sweating as he made eye contact with Amir. His dark stare was full of death. Right then he could see that this guy was not about to be talked down. As these thoughts entered his mind, Amir rolled down the window and unleashed multiple rounds into Agent Smith's body, which thrust him back and briefly sucked the air from his lungs. His body crashed to the ground and knocked the air back into his lungs.

At the same time, Amir got out of the van and yelled, "You Americans will feel the wrath of Allah! Allah u Akbar!"

Before he could press the button on the detonator, the sniper squeezed the trigger and sent a .50 caliber slug through the air, crashing into his head and clearing all thoughts of terrorizing this country forever as his skull erupted and displayed a pink mist of skull and brain matter. His body was left with no reflex other than to fall to the ground lifeless. Multiple agents and airport officers rushed in to see if Agent Smith was all right.

"You okay?" they asked as he was getting up.

"The wind got knocked out of me, and I'll have a few bruises to talk about, but I'm fine. We got that piece of shit and stopped him from killing anyone else," he said, before looking up at the chopper and giving the sniper a thumbs-up for a good shot. A shot that was necessary to save many people's lives.

CHAPTER 27

OVER AT FBI HEADQUARTERS, Agent Johnson was awaiting a call from Rakman. He figured he would call since the news was releasing coverage of what was going on over at the airport. It didn't take long before he called in and wanted answers and revenge for his cousin's demise.

"Agent Johnson speaking, how can I help you?"

"You can't help, so put your boss, Jack Ross, on now!" Rakman demanded. Johnson passed over the phone quickly. He wanted to know what his next move was going be. "Ross here."

"Your men followed my cousin. What is wrong with you people?"

"Nothing is wrong. No one is following your cousin, because he's dead," Jack said, not really wanting him to know much.

But it slipped because of how fed up he was becoming with this terrorist scum.

"You are so stupid to risk the lives of thousands just to capture one man. How much sense does this make to you?" Rakman yelled.

He was beyond pissed that his cousin was unable to fulfill his destiny, but he planned on going through with his acts of terror.

"This country will pay with the blood of thousands, and it will all be on your hands!" he threatened, before he hung up fast, ready to get things done before he too was stopped.

"Agent Johnson, I got him! He's at 1600 Baboli Drive. It's the old Frito-Lay warehouse," the tech said, excited about tracking down the cell signal.

Agent Johnson took a team to that address. They were ready to take him down. Meanwhile, Jack Ross was standing there thinking about the agent and civilian lives that were lost today.

"Keep track of that cell phone signal's movement in case he leaves," Jack Ross said.

"I'm already on it, sir."

Rakman and his team were readying to leave the warehouse. He knew his time was limited. He couldn't trust being at any of his properties or his associates' properties because the FBI was coming hard and fast. He was not trying to stick around for that. He tossed his cell phone on the desk in the office. He had another that he had not used. It was also a burner phone.

Rakman got into his S600 Mercedes Benz, a car he kept at the warehouse for moments like this. It was also where he kept the backup cell phone. He had to be calculated in this business, thinking ahead and having plans A through C. It was something he learned when dealing with his connected associates in powerful places.

As he drove off, he made a call to his soldiers he had in place. He wanted them to know to carry on with the plan if they did not hear from him. The Arab men were in a new all-black cargo van with decals on it.

At 3:00 p.m., the city's baseball team, the Senators, was playing in a packed stadium in City Island. There were more than five thousand fans cheering on their team. However, it was also the same place where the terrorists were, but they came to cheer in the name of Allah by way of Rakman Hussein, the face of evil and death.

The vans fit right in with the Senators' logos on the outside. Each van was parked close to the stadium to maximize the impact of the explosions. If they did it at the same time, it would level the stadium and kill everyone inside. A large enough explosion would perhaps even blow a deep enough hole into the island to cause the water beneath to come through.

At 3:20 p.m. Agent Johnson and his team of agents stormed Rakman's warehouse ready to take him down, but they found nothing. No one was in sight. He did take notice that the warehouse was outfitted to make signs and decals, so that explained how it was so easy for them to get through secured areas.

"Be alert, men. We don't want another incident like before," Agent Johnson said, referring to the previous warehouse with the men inside the office.

The agents fanned out and looked for people as well as information that would lead them to Rakman.

Agent Johnson called it in, since no one was in sight.

"Jack Ross here."

"Sir, we didn't find anyone here. He must have left sooner than we thought."

"I'm looking at the screen, and it's showing the cell signal is still coming from inside the warehouse."

"Be careful, men, his cell signal is still showing

its presence here," Agent Johnson made his men aware. "All right, sir, I'll get back to you if we come across him or something leading to him," he said, ending the call to focus on sweeping the warehouse.

The agents closed in on an office at the back of the warehouse. They entered with caution, not wanting to be ambushed as were the previous agents at the last warehouse. There were many windows in the office, which allowed the agents to glimpse through, yet they found nothing. There was no one inside. The agents decided to go inside the office, where they found the cell phone sitting on the desk.

"Agent Johnson, there's a phone on the desk in here," one of the agents said.

Agent Johnson started walking toward his agents, when a blast and roaring sound soared through the air and thrust his body back. The door to the office was rigged with C-4 explosives that shook the building's structure as the ball of flames and violent force engulfed the agents at the door. Agent Johnson was slammed up against the racks before hitting the ground hard. He briefly went unconscious until the remaining agents' voices could be heard yelling out.

Back at the office, Jack Johnson saw the cell

phone signal disappear, so he knew something was wrong. He called Agent Johnson's phone, only to receive no answer.

"Son of a bitch!" he snapped, upon realizing he may have lost another team of agents. This was not a good look for the country or the bureau.

He called back again; however, this time a voice came across the phone.

"Hello."

"Is everything all right?" he asked.

"Yes, sir, this is Agent Thompson. Johnson is pulling himself together, sir. A bomb went off in the back of the warehouse killing three agents."

Jack Ross could feel the thumping in his chest from his heart beating and being torn from the loss of his men.

"God damn it! This shit has to end!" he said out loud, losing control over his emotions.

It had been a long night and day thus far for this country as well as the bureau.

The call was already out to secure all travel areas. Rakman would not be getting out of this city alive. The ATF, state troopers, national guard, and army were all present. They were all securing the city limits.

"You boys get back here so we can track down this scum."

The call ended, but Jack Ross's thoughts were going one hundred miles an hour. He glanced over at the picture of Rakman and his cousin posted on the board.

"It's not over yet, you piece of scum," he said before he then turned to the agents present. "I want his face on the news. More important, I want all known agencies—local, state, and federal—to have his picture. I don't want him leaving this city; and if he does, I don't want him making his way out of the country."

CHAPTER 28

BY 3:45 P.M. RAKMAN was feeling the heat of the city closing in on him since there were now checkpoints everywhere. He decided to make his way onto the City Island. As he was driving onto the island, there were officers directing the traffic there, too. He couldn't turn back. It was too late now; besides, a U-turn would draw more attention to him. The officers were doing their normal job. It was no different than any other time there was a major event on the island.

Rakman called his men to see if they were in position. He wanted to know what part of the stadium they were at, so he could meet up with them. One of his soldiers picked up.

"My brother, is the time here?" the soldier asked, ready to die.

"We're close. I'm here with you on the island. Where are you?"

"Right side of the stadium."

"Remember, our word will be done at four o'clock," he said, hanging up the phone as he grew impatient, sitting in the long line of cars while waiting on the officer to direct them to go. He yelled out the window, "Let's get this show on the road!"

"You need to wait like everyone else, or I'll leave your ass in traffic!" the female officer said while rolling her eyes.

"You stupid bitch!" Rakman said.

She heard him, so she gave him the finger before continuing on directing traffic.

Another officer came to relieve her for her break.

"Kim, I got it from here. Everything going smooth?"

"No, I just had to put somebody in their place."

"Oh, these pictures just came in, so send them to all the law enforcement. He handed her an 8 x 10 color photo of Rakman Hussein.

"This is that same smart-ass I just checked."

She couldn't believe what she was seeing. At the same time, the male officer who heard her was caught off guard. She looked up from the picture and turned her head in the direction that the S600 Mercedes Benz went. She pointed in the direction where Rakman was parking.

"There's that smart-ass there," she said, pulling out her gun and running toward him.

Unfortunately, she did not read the wanted poster that read to call it in or approach with caution because he was extremely dangerous. The male officer ran behind her, leaving the drivers in traffic to figure it out for themselves.

She came within thirty feet before she yelled out to him.

"Freeze! Freeze asshole!"

When Rakman and his right-hand man saw this, they took cover behind the cars while also taking out their weapons. Rakman was brandishing his twin .45mms. It was time, and he was ready to die.

Around 3:55 p.m. all the officers on the island were doing their routine parameter checks to make sure cars were only parked where they were supposed to. They were also on the lookout for potential auto theft and robbery attempts. They came across a van with a man inside looking down at his phone. The officer tapped on the window to tell him to move since he was in a restricted parking area.

The Arab man suddenly opened fire and sent slugs through the window. He hit the cop and thrust him back as the officer returned fire before hitting the ground.

Back on the other side of the island, Rakman lifted his twin .45mms and squeezed the triggers, allowing the hot melting slugs to race through the barrels. The bullets charged through the air until they met the flesh of the female office running toward him. Her body flipped forward as she grunted, feeling the force from the slugs as well as the heat of the metal melting her flesh. She regrouped quickly because the thought of dying today and leaving her four kids alone was not going to happen. She pulled herself out of harm's way by hiding behind a car.

"I'm going to kill his smart ass," she said while peeping around the car to see Rakman still standing with his guns pointed. She fired off a few rounds, which forced him to take cover. "You're going to jail tonight, muthafucka!" she yelled out in between shooting her weapon.

"You deserve to be shot, you nosey bitch!"

"I can't believe he called me nosey. I'm only doing my job!" she said, seeing her male partner run over and find her up against the car wounded.

"Hey, you good?" he asked.

"Yeah, I'll make it home to my babies, but his smart ass is going to jail if I don't kill him first for shooting me."

"Don't worry about it, I got you," he responded, radioing for backup as well as medical attention for his partner.

He then stood up and took aim, firing at Rakman and his goon before ducking behind the car.

"You should have read the warrant. It says don't approach him like this. He is responsible for the explosions today."

"Well, he ain't going to blow anything else up. His ass is going to jail today!" she said.

CHAPTER 29

ON THE OTHER SIDE of the island, the other Arab member stepped out of his van at precisely 3:57 p.m. to assist his Muslim brother. The two officers were taking cover in between firing off rounds, until one of them raised up to take out the suspect. However, he caught a slug in the neck causing vital damage as he reached for his neck to attempt to stop the blood from spewing out of his neck. Fear came fast as the reality of death set in. He dropped to the ground thinking about the life he had lived up until this point. Seconds later he gasped, taking his last breath as a tear of death slid down his face.

The first officer that was hit in the chest saw this happen to his partner as he jumped up and feared the worst to come for him. His military background kicked in, so he took aim on the Arab men. He controlled his breathing as he pulled the trigger and took out the first of the two men with a precise head shot. The other took cover fast. At the same time, Harrisburg police officers arrived quickly and assisted by cornering the Arab man behind the van.

"Let me see your hands! Don't make any sudden moves or you're dead!" the police officer said, with his adrenaline pumping and mind racing over thoughts of today's events thus far.

The Arab man didn't have any intention of freezing or going to jail. Suddenly, he shifted his weapon on the officer. He wanted to kill them; however, he also knew that they would not hesitate to kill him.

The officers fired on him and sent multiple slugs into his body, sucking the life from his flesh. At the same time, he managed to get a slug off and hit the officer in his arm. The officer was so enraged that he rushed in on the downed man and pumped another round into his face.

"You fucking scumbag! You come into our country terrorizing our people!" he snapped.

Over on the other side of the island, Rakman was still keeping the officers at bay sending slugs whizzing past their heads.

"It'll all be over soon. You Americans never will understand!" he yelled out, upon firing off rounds at the female officer and her partner.

He didn't know his men wouldn't be setting off any explosions on the island today. It was over for explosions today. He and his right-hand soldier were the only ones left on the island.

The island was becoming flooded with local, state, and federal law officials that had now been made aware of the shootout, so Rakman was not going anywhere except to the graveyard from here.

"Brother, I'll try to buy you some time if you want to escape somehow," his right-hand goon said, not even giving Rakman a chance to respond.

He came out from behind the cars and raced toward where the female officer was opening fire.

"Allah u Akbar! I will kill all of you Americans!" he yelled out, pulling the trigger back-to-back.

He didn't even see it coming as multiple bullets rained through the air from multiple officers. His body twisted around as the brute force of the bullets took chunks of his flesh and bones, spraying them everywhere before he hit the ground.

Rakman was checking his clips to see how many rounds he still had remaining, which amounted to only a few left in each gun. After popping the clips back in the check, his watch read 4:10 p.m. Not good, he thought. His men should have detonated the explosives already. The end for him was now, and he knew it. He jumped up firing off rounds at the now-standing female officer. In his last attempt, he turned the gun on himself and shouted, "Allah u Akbar."

He squeezed the trigger. Nothing, he was out of bullets. But it didn't stop the slugs that she sent through the air, slamming into his body, thrusting him back, and knocking the guns out of his hand. He was hit in the arm and shoulder.

The law enforcement closed in fast on Rakman.

"I told you I was going to get you, smart ass," Kim said as she turned him over and placed the cuffs on him until federal agents came over. "We got it from here, ma'am."

"Ma'am? I'm a young thirty. Don't ma'am me. Call me Kim or Officer Wallace."

The agents did not pay her any mind. They were too serious and focused on having Rakman in custody. They immediately called in to make Jack Ross aware of his capture. They also made sure he got medical attention, because he needed to be alive, so America and the city could get the justice they well deserved.

"You think having me in cuffs and custody makes it better or that this is all over? This is just the beginning!" Rakman yelled out, not wanting to accept defeat.

All of the media outlets swarmed the island, trying to be the first to tell their versions of what took place. Their cameras zoomed in on the officers and agents hauling off Rakman.

"Rakman Hussein is the man you see they have in custody. He is also responsible for the acts of terror today. In his million-dollar community, he is a respected neighbor, and in the business world he is an elite and a success. So, you never know who is hiding in our country wanting to terrorize this nation to prove a point they believe is valid. This story will unfold even more because his trial, without question, is going to be a public matter. Right now, the FBI and other agencies will have their hands full in getting information from him to see if others are involved." The female reporter stopped speaking as the cameraman took in the view of the scene around them.

~ ~ ~

I was on the bus looking at the news on the television in the headrest of the seat. I was tripping upon seeing Rakman go down.

"They gotcha, you muthafucka, before I could put a bullet in your head," I said, thinking about how much I wanted to kill this muthafucka for making so many attempts on my life.

One thing I can say is that he fucked up when he sent those fake agents, because now I'm free and on the run, thanks to his bitch ass. It felt better and better the farther this bus took me away from the city. Now I was going to have to stay low but find a team I could trust to make moves to generate money, so I could survive. Because even with the money I had, it was not like I could open a business on the run. I had to put that money back out into the streets to keep making it pop for me. In the meantime, I was going to as lay low as possible until I figured out who I could trust.

While I was getting my thoughts together on the bus, Rico, Chino, Flaco, and Angel were on the highway heading on vacation with the money I gave them. It was the most money they ever had, and they were about to live it up to the fullest.

"Yo, bro, we hood rich for real!" Angel said in excitement about the cash.

"If we play our cards right, we can make this shit flip ten times and have more cash flow, *entiendo*," Rico said, thinking about the future of his crew.

"We're going to grow and build our own shit so the *morenos* and Latinos in our city and state can see we the real deal to fuck with. We just have to stay focused," Rico added.

"I feel you, bro. So, after we get done partying and shit, it's time to get that paper," Flaco said as they took it all in and embraced their newfound riches.

A few weeks later the Feds came to the York County Prison looking for me for a hearing for all of the charges I had received. To their surprise, them fake-ass Feds had already checked me out of the prison, thanks to Rakman's bitch ass. Now the Feds put out an all-points bulletin for me. I was now just like Rakman once was. I was a wanted man, but the plus side for me was that I already had a few weeks' jump on them. I found a low-key spot in Atlanta and blended in at the Thomasville projects, the ghetto of the hood, so I was good down here. This would be my new city. I just had to find a squad of real niggas to get down with. Until then, I'd be staying out of sight and out of mind.

Part Two Now Available

Text Good2Go at 31996 to receive new release updates via text message.

To order books, please fill out the order form below:
To order films please go to www.good2gofilms.com

Name: __ _____

Address:_____

City: _____ State: _____ Zip Code: _____

Phone:_____

Email:_____

Method of Payment: Check   VISA   MASTERCARD

Credit Card#:_ _____

Name as it appears on card: _____

Signature: _____

Item Name	Price	Qty	Amount
48 Hours to Die – Silk White	$14.99		
A Hustler's Dream - Ernest Morris	$14.99		
A Hustler's Dream 2 - Ernest Morris	$14.99		
A Thug's Devotion – J. L. Rose and J. M. McMillon	$14.99		
Black Reign – Ernest Morris	$14.99		
Bloody Mayhem Down South – Trayvon Jackson	$14.99		
Bloody Mayhem Down South 2 – Trayvon Jackson	$14.99		
Business Is Business – Silk White	$14.99		
Business Is Business 2 – Silk White	$14.99		
Business Is Business 3 – Silk White	$14.99		
Childhood Sweethearts – Jacob Spears	$14.99		
Childhood Sweethearts 2 – Jacob Spears	$14.99		
Childhood Sweethearts 3 - Jacob Spears	$14.99		
Childhood Sweethearts 4 - Jacob Spears	$14.99		
Connected To The Plug – Dwan Marquis Williams	$14.99		
Connected To The Plug 2 – Dwan Marquis Williams	$14.99		
Connected To The Plug 3 – Dwan Williams	$14.99		
Deadly Reunion – Ernest Morris	$14.99		
Dream's Life – Assa Raymond Baker	$14.99		
Flipping Numbers – Ernest Morris	$14.99		
Flipping Numbers 2 – Ernest Morris	$14.99		
He Loves Me, He Loves You Not - Mychea	$14.99		
He Loves Me, He Loves You Not 2 - Mychea	$14.99		
He Loves Me, He Loves You Not 3 - Mychea	$14.99		
He Loves Me, He Loves You Not 4 – Mychea	$14.99		
He Loves Me, He Loves You Not 5 – Mychea	$14.99		

Lord of My Land – Jay Morrison	$14.99		
Lost and Turned Out – Ernest Morris	$14.99		
Love Hates Violence	$14.99		
Married To Da Streets – Silk White	$14.99		
M.E.R.C. - Make Every Rep Count Health and Fitness	$14.99		
Money Make Me Cum – Ernest Morris	$14.99		
My Besties – Asia Hill	$14.99		
My Besties 2 – Asia Hill	$14.99		
My Besties 3 – Asia Hill	$14.99		
My Besties 4 – Asia Hill	$14.99		
My Boyfriend's Wife - Mychea	$14.99		
My Boyfriend's Wife 2 – Mychea	$14.99		
My Brothers Envy – J. L. Rose	$14.99		
My Brothers Envy 2 – J. L. Rose	$14.99		
Naughty Housewives – Ernest Morris	$14.99		
Naughty Housewives 2 – Ernest Morris	$14.99		
Naughty Housewives 3 – Ernest Morris	$14.99		
Naughty Housewives 4 – Ernest Morris	$14.99		
Never Be The Same – Silk White	$14.99		
Shades of Revenge – Assa Raymond Baker	$14.99		
Slumped – Jason Brent	$14.99		
Someone's Gonna Get It – Mychea	$14.99		
Stranded – Silk White	$14.99		
Supreme & Justice – Ernest Morris	$14.99		
Supreme & Justice 2 – Ernest Morris	$14.99		
Supreme & Justice 3 – Ernest Morris	$14.99		
Tears of a Hustler - Silk White	$14.99		
Tears of a Hustler 2 - Silk White	$14.99		
Tears of a Hustler 3 - Silk White	$14.99		
Tears of a Hustler 4- Silk White	$14.99		
Tears of a Hustler 5 – Silk White	$14.99		
Tears of a Hustler 6 – Silk White	$14.99		

ALL EYES ON TOMMY GUNZ

The Panty Ripper - Reality Way	$14.99		
The Panty Ripper 3 – Reality Way	$14.99		
The Solution – Jay Morrison	$14.99		
The Teflon Queen – Silk White	$14.99		
The Teflon Queen 2 – Silk White	$14.99		
The Teflon Queen 3 – Silk White	$14.99		
The Teflon Queen 4 – Silk White	$14.99		
The Teflon Queen 5 – Silk White	$14.99		
The Teflon Queen 6 - Silk White	$14.99		
The Vacation – Silk White	$14.99		
Tied To A Boss - J.L. Rose	$14.99		
Tied To A Boss 2 - J.L. Rose	$14.99		
Tied To A Boss 3 - J.L. Rose	$14.99		
Tied To A Boss 4 - J.L. Rose	$14.99		
Tied To A Boss 5 - J.L. Rose	$14.99		
Time Is Money - Silk White	$14.99		
Tomorrow's Not Promised – Robert Torres	$14.99		
Tomorrow's Not Promised 2 – Robert Torres	$14.99		
Two Mask One Heart – Jacob Spears and Trayvon Jackson	$14.99		
Two Mask One Heart 2 – Jacob Spears and Trayvon Jackson	$14.99		
Two Mask One Heart 3 – Jacob Spears and Trayvon Jackson	$14.99		
Wrong Place Wrong Time – Silk White	$14.99		
Young Goonz – Reality Way	$14.99		
Subtotal:			
Tax:			
Shipping (Free) U.S. Media Mail:			
Total:			

Make Checks Payable To:
Good2Go Publishing
7311 W Glass Lane,
Laveen, AZ 85339

CPSIA information can be obtained
at www.ICGtesting.com
Printed in the USA
LVHW031603051218
599370LV00018B/660/P

9 781947 340275